THOU SHALT KILL

A Novel by

PAUL RODRIGUEZ

THOU SHALT KILL

A Novel by

PAUL RODRIGUEZ

A division of Squire Publishers, Inc.
4500 College Blvd.
Leawood, KS 66211
1/888/888-7696

Copyright 2001
Printed in the United States

ISBN: 1-58597-097-2

Library of Congress Control Number: 2001 132863

LEATHERS
PUBLISHING

A division of Squire Publishers, Inc.
4500 College Blvd.
Leawood, KS 66211
1/888/888-7696

Chapter 1

BEING bad can be pretty good. Particularly if you're bad enough, which Snake Ellis most certainly was. Nobody messed with Snake; those who had were either heartily sorry for it, or, as most recently, unfeeling of any emotion at all — ever again. Everyone on the street knew that Snake had knifed a dude who was trying to cut in on his territory, and several people had been squeezed by the police into admitting that they might possibly have seen something; but at the trial, they rightly figured that their testimony wouldn't bring the other dude back to life again. They also rightly figured they probably wouldn't earn any popularity points with either Snake or any of his associates if they testified against him. So they didn't. They suffered from convenient lapses of memory as to what the alleged murderer allegedly looked like, and they couldn't be sure it was Snake. In fact, come to think of it, it didn't look like Snake after all. So Snake was still on the street, and all their hides were unperforated. Which was just the way they liked them.

And, in keeping with their strong respect for individual liberties, nobody forced their companionship on Snake as he walked out the door of Shakie's Social Center and Bar-B-Q. So it happened that Snake stood there all alone on the front steps, having a cigarette and reflecting upon last month's acquittal and this month's inventory of recreational chemicals. Snake hadn't heard of the old slogan, "better living through chemistry," but if he had, he'd have appropriated it for his own use — violently.

He saw, but dismissed the nun walking slowly toward him. Nuns didn't walk around this neighborhood very much. Nuns didn't walk around here at all. But if she wanted to get mugged, that was her business. As she drew nearer, their eyes made contact. She raised her left hand, holding a brightly polished crucifix and softly murmured, "This is for you, Mr. Ellis."

As Snake's eyes focused on the shining metal, he missed her right hand coming out of the folds of her habit, and the sawed-off 20-gauge shotgun in it. Snake's last thought was unformed when it disappeared in a flash of light he didn't get to see.

The nun dropped both hands and spun around into the alleyway, out of the dim wash of light from Shakie's window. As she walked through to the cross-alley to the south side of the block, she drew a shopping bag from under her robes. In less than thirty seconds her habit joined the shotgun in the shopping bag. One minute later, an old woman rounded the corner in time to see the first customers cautiously spilling out of the bar. She stood at the edge of the crowd for a moment, then nodded and silently walked away, just as the low notes of a siren started up in the distance. Emma Schechter walked slowly toward the nursing home where she lived, carrying her burden, a filled shopping bag.

* * * * * * * * *

"So where the hell do we go from here, Dan?" Lew looked down at the body on the sidewalk, lit another cigarette off the previous one, and pitched the butt into the gutter. It was late in their shift, and they hadn't really needed to catch this squeal. Now it was after their shift, but since the squeal had been theirs, they got to stay on the job. Long on the job. Lew recalled some cop a long time ago telling him about a unique corollary to Murphy's Law, which went, "the later in your shift, the more likely you are to catch a major squeal." Bigger'n hell, that old cop had been right.

"Hell if I know, man," Dan answered, "I'm just a dumb street cop. Let's do the routine, see if we can get lucky, maybe even find some dude inside with a shotgun in his sleeve and smoke coming out his collar." His voice dropped: "Anyway, we can be thankful there's one less badass to worry about. I knew this dude here, before I even pulled his ID. Name's Henry Ellis, street name's Snake. Thoroughly bad. Walked on a murder-one about a month ago. Odds

2

are, somebody offed him for watcha-call-yer-basic professional reasons, anyway."

So they did the routine. After the crime scene work, the routine consisted of directing the police photographer to do his thing, asking the M.E.'s boys to do their thing, and trying to get even one witness to do his or her thing. Two out of three ain't bad, someone once said. The interviews all went like this:

"What did you hear?"

"I didn't hear nothin', man."

"Well, what did you see?"

"I didn't see nothin', man."

"Bullshit. You tellin' me you're blind?"

"No, man, I just didn't see anythin'."

"Well, do you know who he was?"

"No, man, I don't think I ever saw him before."

"Okay, where were you when this happened?"

"I wasn't nowhere, man."

"What the hell you mean, you wasn't nowhere? Everybody's somewhere, now where the hell were you?"

"I was in the restroom, man, takin' a leak."

"Yeah, right, well, what's your name?"

"I ain't nobody, man."

And so it went. Forty-three non-persons, including the bartender, were in the same restroom, simultaneously taking a leak when Snake Ellis was transported from this world.

"You through playing games with these people, let's take them all in, sweat them for a while, maybe see what drips out?" Lew suggested.

Dan paused, thoughtful. "Naw, there's no percentage. Besides, every one of them's a former customer, one way or the other. We want their names, we've already got them. This one's not gonna come directly, and sure as hell, not from them. Let's get out of here."

Dan turned and shot twelve thousand volts of evil eye down the bar. It bounced off the backs and sides of heads, since not one was turned in their direction. "And the same to you, brothers," he murmured, as he turned to leave.

They were two steps down, one from the sidewalk, when the magic volume switch turned on, and voices hummed from inside

3

the bar. They made the sidewalk, their shoes blurring the chalked man-shaped outline as they stepped on it, when the jukebox turned back on.

Dan Perkins and Lew Perkins were a team. They'd been partnered for almost three years, after the vagaries of a duty roster had placed them in alphabetic order. Each had just lost a partner, Lew's to a bullet, Dan's to a heart attack in the Police Department's gym. They were roughly the same height, weight and age. Apart from those facts, almost nothing about them matched.

Dan was a brilliant, almost academic intellectual, with a tendency toward street slang retained from his youth in the ghetto in Detroit, and a casual cynicism used to conceal his true thoughts. Dan could also be a non-linear thinker, jumping from A to E with no stops in between, and was equipped with a memory like a filing cabinet.

Lew was an uncomplicated thinker, who had to work through B, C and then D before also getting to E.

Dan's wardrobe tended toward the flashy, often causing Lew to refer to it as "conservative pimp." Lew's lack of concern for the niceties of dress, on the other hand, allowed Dan to refer to him as one who'd get thrown out of a winos' convention for not coming up to the dress code.

A few things about them, though, made them good partners. Each respected the other's capabilities; both passionately believed in the value of what they were doing; they had learned to anticipate each other's moves; and, most of all, each complemented the other in a synergistic way that had been best expressed by another detective: "Those two guys make a three-man team."

As they drove back downtown through the still crowded streets on this Friday night, Lew talked to himself, trying to arrange his thoughts.

"This makes, what, eight, nine people offed, all but one that I can think of shot, all bad guys, long-time hoods and low-lifes. All within four, five months, all without witnesses, all with potential motives for somebody to knock them off from here to Sunday. They're serial murders, Dan, no doubt about it, but who's doing it? Are we looking at some kind of mob thing, maybe a takeover for their action? Hell, these guys're pretty long shots to be connected. They're

4

into various kinds of rackets, we got hoods, pimps, pushers, armed robbers, killers, mob guys, we got shit, is what we got. There's diddley to connect them with each other. So, who? Why? What gives?"

Dan slouched back down in the front seat, re-aimed the air conditioner vent, and softly cursed the tepid air that came out. There ought to be a law says P.D. cars can't roll without amenities, he thought. He rearranged his tie, all the while scanning the outside world to his right, noticing the patterns of street life in the sodium-vapor day of this late hour, unconsciously looking for the breaks in the rhythm that suggested something going down out there. "You got me, Bro, but I can tell you I'm not sure do I like it or not. One, somebody's literally getting away with murder. Last I heard, that's still illegal. Two, somebody's offing nobody but bad guys, of whom we have a surplus anyway. Sort of the social version of urban renewal. Society's better off without these dudes."

"We once had a hell of an argument in one of my courses, my senior year at the U, over something like this. The class pretty well broke into two groups over was it a good or bad thing. Criminology prof wasn't much help, either. Never did get any straight answers on it. So I came to my own conclusion. Even wrote my last term paper in Criminal Law on it. I called it, are you ready for this? I called it, Laudable Homicide, advocated reverse trials, where the killer had to prove he'd done it before he could collect. See, I had a graduated series of awards postulated, for civic service, based upon how bad the dead cat was. I figured, what the hell, if you could go up from Murder One, through Murder Two, through accidental homicide, through the various degrees of manslaughter and justifiable, why not top the list off with something you could get rewarded for? Really messed over that prof's mind. He was one of those chic ultra-liberals, figured police work was just too, too awful, how it oppressed minorities, and all that. He had a bad time with me, just not understanding that a black man might not like the shit he was putting out. His idea was to blame it all on society and the government, and ignore the possibility that there's any decision-making going on in the street. Dumb shit. But, my man, his kind of thinking did have its advantages. I Mau-Mau'd him into giving me an A for the course."

The easy tones of his voice became more clipped, as he tensed.

"Go slow, Bro, and check the red shirt there wearing the white felonies, under the street light. He's about to go for that woman's purse. Get ready." Lew eased over to the right a little, lifted his foot off the accelerator and mentally started the count. At the count of seven, the perpetrator made his grab at the purse. At the count of eight, Dan was out of the car. At eleven, two expensively slacked knees rested on the perp's kidneys, as he sucked sidewalk.

"Now, little Bro," Dan said, "let me tell you about your rights. You got the right to be silent, my man, and you got the right to have your lawyer with you during any questioning my partner, yeah, the white guy here, and me may want to do. You dig? If you can't afford no lawyer, the city'll even pop for one for you. You got that? See, Babe, you even got the right to know that anything you do say, it can and it will be used against you in a court of law. We straight? Good."

"But you can forget it all, my man, 'cause what we got here is, we got two po-lice officers who observed you do the crime, and we ain't got nooooo questions for old lucky here. Nope, none at all, Baby, you just lost this one cold. Now, my man, these here cuffs don't feel none too tight, do they? Good. Mind your head, now, gettin' in the car."

* * * * * * * * *

Snake's neighborhood was just about what they'd expected, what had once been fairly good-sized mansions, that had gone to seed maybe forty years ago and had been cut up into smaller apartments. Along both sides of the streets, about half of the cars looked as if they would never run again. Most of them had at least one flat tire and a few had no wheels at all. Dan pulled into a parking spot, hoping he could miss the broken glass in the gutter. He didn't hear anything crunch under his front wheel, so he smiled. "Well, we're here, partner."

"Yeah, Lew murmured, as he looked around. "Question is, where the hell is here?"

"Low rent district, my man. This here's where ol' Snake got his next-of-kin stashed. You ready to come all the way awake, or shall I go do this, an' leave you a wake-up call? I mean, I can handle this if you want me to."

"Bullshit. You leave my ass here, they'll steal me along with the hubcaps. Nope, I might as well go with you." Lew rolled his shoulders one more time, trying to ease the pain radiating downward. Got to get rid of that mattress, he thought. "Besides, I'm awake now. Got to keep an eye on you."

As they walked back down the street to the gray stuccoed house, Dan murmured low, "Not hardly what you'd expect from a dude carries rolls of hundreds around in his pockets, is it? Pisses me off, my man; here we are, doin' it in the street every day, busting scumballs like that Snake, and they got our whole salary wrapped up in one rubber band. Man, we are in the wrong freakin' business."

"You're right, Dan," Lew answered, "The hell with this. I quit. So do you. From now on, let's be dealers. No, wait a minute. Let's be wholesalers, maybe even importers. That's it, let's set up as international kingpins. We'll import half of Colombia, maybe buy us a couple of cities, declare ourselves independent. How's that strike you?"

"Right on, my man, right on. From now on, nothin' but the high life. We hit the Riviera in the winters, the Hamptons in the summers. By the way, where the hell are the Hamptons?"

"Shit, I don't know. Hey, tell you what; until we find out where the Hamptons are, just in case we don't want to go there, let's stay cops for just a little longer, all right?"

Dan shrugged. "Well, all right, if you want to, what the hell's a few days more? Here we go, apartment B."

There was no answer at apartment B. Not for the first knock, the second, or the third, which was more fist pounding than knocking. C, however, opened a crack. "You cops? Who you want?"

"Miz Ellis."

"She don't live here no more."

"When'd she move?"

"What'd she do?"

Dan lowered his voice to the don't-mess-with-me level. "I said, when'd she move?"

"Month, maybe two. Don't nobody live there now."

"How'd you know?"

"Seen 'em go." Click.

There being no answers to delicate, or even violent pounding on any of the other doors, they walked off the porch, blinking into the sudden sunlight.

"This sucks."

"Yeah."

"Postoffice?"

"Yeah."

"Goddamnit, Dan, stop that. Now we're all talking in monosyllables. I recommend, my friend, that we proceed to the Yewnited States Post Office, whereat we shall inquire of the Postmaster, if any person or persons, using the surname Ellis, shall have, recently, or in the past few months, registered a change of address, for the purpose of forwarding such mail as may have been sent them through postal channels. You got that?

"Yeah."

At the branch post office Lew walked the short maze to the window, admiring the portraits of felons on the wall, casting a critic's eye on the commemorative stamps advertised next to them, and at the brightly colored cartoon characters printed on neckties for sale. "You believe this? Cartoon neckties? What the hell ever happened to stamps, boxes, Zip Code directories, and all the traditional stuff you're supposed to find in post offices, anyway?

"Market share, my man," Dan answered. "You go with the flow, you sell what sells, you make a little profit, your stamps don't cost so much, 'cause you've diversified. Yep, I think the soda fountain could go over here, the deli over there, and the latte machine in the corner."

The clerk looked at the badges, unimpressed. "Happy to help. gentlemen, just fill out this form, and we'll go look at the register." Dan sighed, pulled out a pen, cross-checked his notes, and wrote down the information he had. "Will this do? Why do we have to go through all this? Why can't you just look, tell us what we want to know, and we'll be on our way."

"Gentlemen, this is the Postal Department. We have rules. We have regulations. We have policies. We have forms. We do things according to the Postal Manual. The Manual says you fill out this form, you fill out this form. I don't make the rules around here, I just go by 'em. Okay?" The clerk walked through the doorway behind him, muttering to himself.

"Watch it, Dan," Lew said. "Don't get him disgruntled. All we got between us is a couple of dozen rounds, and there's no telling what he may have. Howitzer or something back there."

Before Dan could respond the clerk was back. "Sorry, no luck, nothing in the records, as far back as a year ago. The route carrier does that route was back there, I also checked with him. Far as he can remember, he's never delivered anything to that address but junk mail, stuff addressed to "Occupant."

"How's he know that?" Dan asked. The clerk leaned an elbow on the counter, and drummed his fingers. "You do a route long enough, you know names, you know addresses, you know return addresses. You know who gets what magazines, what bills, letters from wherever, you get so you know a lot. We don't open them, we don't read them, we don't do anything but deliver, but I'll bet right now your route carrier, did I ask him, could tell me all about you, maybe more than you'd want him to know. Trust me; if he says he never delivered any real mail, he never delivered any real mail."

Dan and Lew said thanks, and turned to go. As they left the counter, the clerk called. "Hey!"

They turned. "What?"

"We got a special on ties. Want one?"

Chapter 2

IN the lobby of Saint Jude's hospital, Emma Schechter looked around, favorably impressed by the pastels and brights she saw splashed all over the walls. The thought passed through her mind that anyplace so nicely decorated must be pleasant, and, therefore, a good hospital. Then a wry thought ran across her consciousness that however good this hospital might look, most of her neighbors didn't leave it alive. She shook off the thought, reminded herself that she was here to be helpful and cheerful, and ambled across the lobby to the information desk. A few questions later, she went into the bright blue elevator, walked along the yellow, white and green hallway, followed the sun-yellow ceiling through a right turn, and found room B-318-A. At the door she paused, cocked her head and softly called into the room, "Yoohoo, hello, anybody in there?"

From the second bed Louise Harcroft replied, "Emma! Come in, come in, it's so good to see you."

Emma sat in the chair by the bed, placed her shopping bag beside the chair and pulled out a skein of yarn, two knitting needles and a box of chocolates, which she placed on the bedside stand. "I brought you these to help keep your spirits up. Eat."

"Sorry, Emma, my blood sugar's up again. Nothing for me, I'm afraid, for quite a while. They say it'll make me sick ... What am I saying? Here I am, 84 years old, and some 30-year-old doctor wants to take away my pleasures? When he's 84 he can tell me how to live that long. Besides, what's left that I haven't done? Now, tell me, what's in these red square ones?"

For the remainder of visiting hours, Emma's knitting needles clicked as she chatted, telling Louise all the latest gossip at the nursing home and adding her own acerbic commentary. At last the talk turned to Louise. Emma put her knitting needles down, reached over and held Louise's worn hands. "Now, don't you worry about a thing, Louise, I'll take care of everything for you. Don't you concern yourself with anything but getting well. We miss you, and we're looking forward to having you come home again."

Louise sighed. "Oh, Emma, I worry so, even when I know I really shouldn't. Did you take care of my fish?" she asked.

"Yes, dear, that nice Mister Belsen cleans their water, and I feed them. They're doing just fine."

"And did you take care of my birds? You know how they are about fresh seed every single morning."

"Yes, dear, I take very good care of the birds. I like them; I may even get one for myself." Her voice dropped to barely audible tones as she said, "And I even took care of ..... the other thing for you, you know."

"Oh, Emma, I'm sorry to be such a bother, I really wanted to take care of that myself."

"Well, don't you bother yourself about it," Emma soothed, "my rotation just came up sooner is all, and, well, there'll be others for you to take care of. After all," her voice dropped almost to a whisper, "there're a lot of THEM out there. There's more than enough to go around."

* * * * * * * * *

Down in the hollow, the sun sets earlier than anywhere else in the park. Which is probably why people don't go there after dark, or even near sundown. Anybody stupid enough to get caught down there deserves to get robbed. Which is the best that can happen to them. The worst that can happen to them generally does. So it was only natural that the three members of Satan's Sons, nattily togged out in their colors, regarded the old man sitting there on the park bench with the blanket wrapped Indian-style around his shoulders as perfectly fair game. Besides, there wasn't anyplace for him to go, since the bench was backed up against a tall wall that stretched like open arms to his left and right. Since this wasn't a public park at all, but the Satan's Sons' private property, the old man would quite naturally have to pay rent for its use. Pretty obvious, when you thought about it, which apparently wasn't what the old man was doing at all. Not at all. So that meant he had to be taught a lesson.

Bad Sugar Martin moved slightly to the left, Tripod D'Angelo moved slightly to the right, and Slick Willy took center spot, as befitted the senior Son. "Hey, old man, what it is, see, is, we need some bread. You dig? We got stuff to do. Now, give it up, and you don't get hurt. After all, we're nice guys, you know?"

Slick smiled and held his hand out. "Yeah, you old fart," Bad Sugar chimed in, "Hurry up. We ain't got all day, man, we got business to take care of."

In a soft voice, the old man asked quietly, "You boys want my money?"

"You got it, Pops, now hurry up."

The old man's gaze swept across the three, very closely, very slowly, and in an even lower voice, he said, "All right, you can have what I've got, if that's what you want."

"Now you got the idea, old man, you ain't so dumb after all."

"Yeah, you old fart, give," Slick said.

A hand moved under the blanket, and the last thing Slick saw was a steel circle, exactly forty-five hundredths of an inch across the hole in the middle. He never registered the flame, about the size of a basketball, that followed the slug out of the barrel.

Bad Sugar froze long enough for a well-rehearsed move to put a bullet into the center of his chest. His last conscious thought was, "Shit, I can't breathe." The bullet that drove its way out the back of his jacket gave Satan a third red eye, visible for only a moment before Bad Sugar toppled backward.

Tripod's reflexes were always fast. That was how he'd managed to win so many fights, the fact that his hands were so good. His hands were so good, in fact, that he was able to reflexively bring both fists in front of him before the third shot. Not that it did him any good, since the bullet went right between them and severed his spinal cord on its way out the back of his neck. He fell backward into a sitting position, then bent forward like a broken doll, his limp fists now in his lap.

Howard Kirk put the GI pistol in the back of his belt, just as he'd carried it all through the infantry campaigns in Europe so many years ago. He pulled the bulky green wool sweater down over it and, walking swiftly now, folded the blanket as he made his way out of the hollow, heading for the street. Once clear he walked more slowly, breathing deeply, slowing his heartbeat and praying this wouldn't bring on another heart attack. At 75, after all, you couldn't be too careful about your health. His hand found its way to the pill bottle in his pants pocket, and he wondered for a moment whether a nitroglycerine pill wouldn't be a good idea.

At the bus stop, just another old man in a green wool sweater climbed aboard the crosstown bus and sat down in a vacant seat. He smiled back at a three-year old staring at him over its mother's shoulder.

* * * * * * * * *

Lew stood up from the body he was examining and started walking up out of the hollow, up the hill toward the memorial tower that stood looking out over the downtown area. He lit a cigarette and stood there, absently flicking the top of his old Zippo open and closed. Something was going on in his city, something he didn't understand. There was no handle on these killings, no common denominator — no linkage to put any of these killings into perspective. Or, at least, as far as he could see, there wasn't. But when you've been a cop long enough, you stop being very surprised at the things people will do to one another. Something you've never seen before becomes just another part of your education. You just accept it, learn from it, file it away, and try to walk away from it when it's over. You do your job as best you can. Most of the time it isn't too difficult. Most people who get murdered, for instance, usually die at the hands of someone they know. Best bet? A relative or acquaintance. Very rarely a total stranger, unless the killing takes place as part of a holdup. But these, these were something else. People killed, without exception, out of their homes, at least so far, almost always somewhere casual, almost every time a public place, and never any witnesses. Spooky.

Even in these times of violence, Lew thought, this city had never had more than its share. This wasn't a particularly comforting idea;

statistically, the city was always a little light on homicides, violent crimes, arsons. Not very comforting if you happened to be a victim, but it was the sort of thing that the mayor, the city council, even the Chamber of Commerce used as a key point. This was one of the very last of what they called the "livable cities."

It had started out as a jumping-off place for the wagon trains going westward and had later become a hub of railroad activity. In those days, you could come here and transfer from one railroad to any other, from one stage line to any other; you could go to almost any part of the country from here. During those times, the great cattle drives had come up from Texas, aimed at the main railheads here. The population changed over the years, almost the same way the rest of the country had. First the Indians, then the trappers, then the settlers, then the migrants, moving through on their way to wherever it was that they'd heard the last rumor about. When the war rolled through, most people weren't sure whose side they were on. The terms North and South both belonged "back East," somehow. What fighting went on was mainly guerrilla-style and largely based upon personal hatreds. After the war, those who stayed built their civilization, bringing with it those driven to build, as well as those willing to tear down. Preachers and outlaws, lawyers, teachers, robber barons, all intent on their own visions.

Along with the frontier heritage and the commerce brought by the railroads, there came violence. It was normal and natural, a part of the times and a part of the personalities of the men (and, in some cases, the women) strong enough to make their lives in this land. There was a time when a man might as well have gone out without his pants as without a gun. It was a part of the fabric of life. Oddly enough, Lew mused, the fact that it was utterly routine for people to walk the streets armed made it less likely that they would be attacked. It was an article of faith among those who prowled the dark corners of the city that there was an inherent danger in making a play on someone who might shoot you dead. So, violence was largely restricted to wars, barroom brawls, occasional knifings and the very occasional shooting.

Lew recalled that there had once been a trial of a man accused of murder, which had become such a celebrated case that the Eastern papers had picked it up and used it as an illustration of how the wild West was uncouth, rough and uncivilized.

Of the facts, there was little doubt and almost no discussion. One Hugh Claxton had been drinking all day and had continually called out a former Union officer named Rodrigo Roberts, whom he'd called, among other things, a "turncoat Texican scoundrel and a coward to boot." Roberts, who'd taken abuse all afternoon and had been pursued by Claxton from place to place, had had enough. He walked out into the street where Claxton now stood brandishing a rifle, calmly drew and shot Claxton through the heart at a distance of about 20 feet.

Roberts' defense attorney would later go on to Congress and would achieve fame for a civil suit concerning a farmer's pet dog, but his first notoriety came when he achieved the acquittal of his client. He convinced the jury that Claxton needed killing and had been considerably improved thereby.

The New York press particularly had a field day poking fun at this rude cowtown, and it remained a favorite characterization by the East in general. For almost a 120 years, everybody east of the Hudson knew that gunfighters, cowboys, war-painted Indians, buffalo, longhorns and unimprisoned murderers roamed the city's mud streets.

Lew's revery was broken by a sleek corporate jet turning final overhead, aiming for the airport adjacent to downtown. He scanned back to the south, looking down at the ring of headlights, flashers, rotating beacons and the portables which threw cold white light on the scene, making it look like some movie set. Except that it was for real. Those were real dead down there, and there was one or more real killers somewhere, thinning out the city's population. He sighed, flicked the butt away and walked back down.

"Where the hell did you go, Bro?" Dan asked.

Lew squatted back down with him, next to the taped outline. "Thinking. And damn unsuccessful at that. How're we here?"

"Coming along. We got three empty shell casings, .45 caliber, maybe a bullet left in one dude here. The others were through-and-through, and no chance of figuring out where the hell they went. Position of the brass suggests one shooter, maybe sitting on the bench here, or standing in front of it. My guess is sitting; looks like the bullets went upward. Guy had to be pretty good though, getting all three of these dudes with one shot each. I'd say he had to have real fast reflexes, too. None of these poor bastards had a chance to turn around and run for it. Except for the fact that the caliber's too big, I'd almost mark this for a mob hit."

"Yeah, but what would the mob want from them? Why would the mob want to come down on three small-change street punks?"

Dan shrugged. "Don't ask me, man, I'm too dumb to answer them, I only ask them."

As Lew stood up, grunting with the effort, a crime scene technician called to him from the bench. "Hey, Perkins, c'mere a minute."

Dan turned and asked, "Which one?"

"Shit, I don't care, all you detectives look alike anyway."

"Smart-ass," Lew mumbled, then moved to the bench.

"Check this out. See here, these fibers, how they're caught under some wood splinters?"

"Yeah, so what?"

"So this: It rained all last night, and it quit, like, say, noon, right? Right. So, these fibers here, they don't show any signs of having been wet. Odds are, these're today's, maybe this evening's. You come up with your killer, ask him if he's got a jacket, sort of greyish-green. After we get this down to the lab, we'll tell you what the makeup is. Maybe get you a little closer."

"Yeah, thanks," Lew said. "We'll get back to you on that."

"No charge, man, part of the service."

Lew turned back. "Well, I'll go over and start with the crowd over there, maybe somebody saw something, heard something, whatever. By the way, who reported it?"

"Little old guy over there with the dog," a uniformed officer chimed in. "He was walking his dog, crested the hill over there, saw these three all sprawled out. Said he got close enough to see all the blood, then hustled over to the Safeway and phoned it in. Like to chewed my ear off, telling me how he found 'em and made the call. He must have told me six times, easy, going over it again and again. Hell, it's probably the most exciting thing ever happened in his life, so I guess maybe he's entitled, huh?"

"Yeah, well," Lew answered, "I might as well give him a shot at telling it for the seventh."

The old man was obviously pleased with all the attention, and

Lew made it a point to use a respectful, you're-very-important tone of voice as he questioned him, to draw him out. As he found out, it wasn't necessary to draw him out.

"Now, Mister, uh, McMorriss, would you tell me exactly what you saw, sir? I know you've already told the officer about this, but maybe you'll tell me one more time, so I'll have it straight in my mind. Please."

"Charlie. Name's Charlie McMorriss. Sure, I'll go over it again," he said. "See, I live about eight blocks from here, at the Forest Fen. It's sort of a retirement home, you see. Well, I like to take Sugar here for pretty long walks. It keeps her fit and does pretty fine for me, too. I can walk the legs off a lot of young folks, you know. They don't walk anyplace. Drive all the time. Makes 'em weak. Wouldn't surprise me, did their kids come with no legs at all, just wheels hung on their backsides. Kids're soft these days, not like in the old days when I was coming up, I can tell you. Anyway, I took Sugar out as usual, and we decided to walk over here. To the park, once around, back home, works out to about three miles. We came into the park through the Oak Street gate, walking along this path here. When we came over the top there," he pointed, "I could see the three kids laying there in the path. I thought they were drunk or something, and I wasn't too sure we shouldn't turn around and walk away, but something about them looked funny. They didn't move or anything, and it all seemed kind of still. Anyway, after they didn't move for about a minute more, I walked a little closer.

"Soon as I got near enough, I could make out the blood. That was as far as I went. I decided I shouldn't touch anything so I wouldn't mess up any clues." He winked. "I learned that from watching television detective stories. Get my fingerprints all over them kids, you might think I had something to do with this. Pretty good, huh? Well, anyway, as soon as I saw what it was all about, I took Sugar with me over to the Safeway store on the other side of the park, and I called the 911 number. Pretty nifty, that 911, I didn't even have to use a dime. That was when I called. Then I walked back here, just in case. I suppose I could have just gone home and all, but I wanted to be here, just in case. You know, in case you needed anything from me. I was first here, after all; wouldn't have been here except for Sugar here. We like to get our daily walk. We started out at the house, and we walked all this distance. It's good for her. Keeps her fit. Does pretty good for me, too. Did I tell you that I can walk the legs off a lot of these younger kids?"

Lew cut in before McMorriss could rerun his adventure. "Yes, sir, you did. Now, can you tell me anything about what you heard, was there any noise, say, like a car backfiring, or anything?"

"No, nothing like that, we didn't hear anything. We just came walking in from the Oak street gate, came over the top there ..."

"Uh, yeah, thank you, Mr. McMorriss, I think I've got it." Lew backed up a couple of steps. "We don't want to hold you up any longer, sir, thanks for your help." He backed up a couple of more steps. "If there's anything we need, we'll contact you. Thank you, sir, have a good day."

Lew started to turn away and then caught what he'd just said. Have a good day? Jeez, did I say that? Some old fart walking his dog comes across the OK Corral here, and I tell him to have a good day? Here's blood and gore spattered all over, and I tell him to have a good day. Right, yeah.

Lew watched as the technicians finished up. The Medical Examiner's men had trundled the bodies away by now, and all the evidentiary items had been collected and tagged. Dan was holding an assortment of blackjacks, sharpened screwdrivers and a small pistol. "Here's their armory, Bro. Except for the Saturday Night Special, all the rest of this shit could've been explained away to some wide-eyed bleeding heart. 'Hell, screwdrivers and small pipe wrenches, they ain't weapons, officer, they're just tools, left over from when I was fixing my car this morning. I just forgot to put 'em back in my tool box.' There's nothing left for us to do here, Lew, what say we wrap this up? I got a lady waiting, or maybe not waiting any more. Either way, man, I am bushed. You?"

"Yeah, I've had it, too," Lew answered.

The trip back downtown held no excitement. The write-up on the initial and pending went quickly, with no major distractions. File folders were made up, stat sheets went into the stat sheet tray, file folders into the active drawer, and two tired cops exited the building only two hours late.

* * * * * * * * *

Sometimes being a cop isn't the greatest job in the world. You may be able to leave the job, but the job doesn't always leave you. Which is why, on this nice September afternoon, Lew and Dan were particularly annoyed to overhear the following conversation from the booth directly behind their own at Ambler's Good Foodery:

"How much can you handle?"

"Maybe two ounces, man. Depends on how good it is."

"This's good, I guarantee. It's damn near pure. Step on it two, three times, it'll still do good."

Lew put down his fork with extreme care, looked at Dan and shrugged. Dan's eyebrows raised ever so slightly, his eyeballs rolling up and around, making up his "oh, shit" expression. One finger held in the air served as communication to wait for more of what Lew's mentally rehearsed testimony would refer to as "reasonable cause to convince us that a criminal act, pertaining to narcotics or other controlled substances, was taking place within our hearing in the next booth."

So Dan sneaked a last sip of coffee as a voice said, "Okay, take this for now. Make a deal on this much, meet me later and we'll work out some more. Just be careful, man, there's a lot of narcs out. One more thing, guy, this's strictly C.O.D., you dig?"

Lew moved first, easing out of the booth, then pivoting quickly as Dan came around his outside, blocking the remainder of the booth. From where he was standing over them, it was easy to keep his voice low and almost conversational, except for the content of what he was saying: "Police Officers. You're both under arrest. Just keep your hands where I can see them. Out slow, you first."

"Yeah, little guy," said Dan in a menacing growl, "you just screwed up our lunch. Now we're gonna screw up your whole day. Real slow now, you make a bad move and I'm gonna remember you made me miss dessert. And then I'm gonna hurt you real bad. Dig?"

Once outside, they put the two young men against the wall. "You know the routine, get your feet further back." The search yielded two switchblade knives, a total of four bags of "unidentified white powdery substance" and two student ID cards from a local high school.

"You shoulda stayed in class today, children," Dan said, " 'cause now you get worse than just an 'F' for the day. Now you got a 'B,' my child, 'B' for busted. Which probably don't mean crap no more, 'cause you just done quit bein' students. You, my heroes, done become perpetrators. What it is, babes," Dan's voice took on a flat, dead tone, "is you just made the big time." As Dan placed handcuffs on them, Lew pulled a small card from a slot in his badge case, and read; "You have the right to remain silent. If you give up the right …"

* * * * * * * * * *

"Well, shit, will you look at that!" Dan diverted his attention from his customers in the back seat and looked through the windshield. At least 20 people were spilling out into the street in front of them, their attention fixed straight up. The recognition was instant. "Jumper," Lew said. "Pull it over here. Looks like we're first .. Jesus, this's gonna be a busy day."

It took only a matter of seconds for Lew and Dan to slip an extra pair of handcuffs to each boy's ankle and around a bar welded to the floor of the unit. "Now, you boys stay right here and don't go wanderin' off, y'hear?"

"Fuck you, pig, I hope you get run over," was all one had time to say before he was talking to a closed door.

The ride to the tenth floor took an eternity. Elevators don't care whether you have a badge or not. In fact, just as an act of mechanical insolence, it chose to stop at the sixth and eighth floors, where nobody got on anyway. At the tenth, they hurried to the office at the end of the hall, pushing their way through the horde of spectators. At the door they paused, took in the situation and unwillingly remembered the last time. Last time it had been a man, despondent over something. They'd never found out what. Nor would they.

When you work with a partner for three years, you begin to know not only his moves, you learn his abilities, his chain of thoughts and his fears. It passed through Lew's mind that this would have to be his action. Dan's worst fear was acrophobia. He wouldn't freeze up, but he'd have that fear working against him, slowing him down, making him overly cautious, less dependable. At the window Lew stopped and called out softly. "Can we talk about this, Ma'am?"

"There's no talking to do. I've already made up my mind. I'm getting off this world once and for all, and this is the best way to do it."

21

"Whoa, wait a second. I'm just going to poke my head out the window so we can talk. That won't hurt anything, will it?" Lew placed his hands on the window sides, then eased his head out. "Here, see? No tricks, no grabs, no heroics. I don't mind telling you, lady, I'm pretty scared just doing this. All I want to do is talk."

He sized up his target: 40, maybe 45, well dressed, reasonably attractive, no shoes, no rings. The shoes were normal; he'd never heard of a woman jumper who wore shoes on the way out. No particular reason, just one of those things, same as the fact that women who shoot themselves rarely go for a head shot like men do, even more rarely put it into their faces, and usually go for the heart. But only after carefully moving their clothing aside. It was just something they do. Something else they do when they jump is they never land gracefully.

"Please, lady, let's talk about it. You can always jump, but please, let's talk it over first. What about your family?"

"My kids are grown, and my husband's long gone. Bastard cleaned me out and split with some young chickie."

"OK, " Lew said, "so that's the reason to do this?"

"It's part of it," she spat, "I'm just tired of all the bullshit. And if you reach for me, I'm going now."

"Uh, uh, no way, lady, I'm not into those games. Did I tell you before that I'm a cop? Well, I am. Hey, look, I'm being up front with you. I don't want you to jump. I see enough misery each day, I don't need to see more. Let's just talk, huh? You got plenty of time to get it done if that's what you really want, but maybe there's another way. You got time."

She looked fully at him for the first time now, with an expression on her face that Lew had seen before, and it chilled him. He recalled Vietnam, seeing men coming in from the bush with that look. They called it the Thousand Yard Stare, as they had through three previous wars. It was a look beyond pain, beyond life. It was the look of the dead. Some people never lost it.

"Look, it's all over, so stop bothering me. Let me get on with it."

An irrational burst of annoyance drove through him. He choked it down, and with a voice as calm and reasonable as he could manage, he started again. "Just wait, give me a minute. Hell, you can spare me a minute, can't you? Will you do that for me? Please? I'm not gonna psych you or play games with your head. No way, I'm not into that. I'm just a street cop, trying to do my job. You want to hear something good? I heard about a cop in New York, pulled his gun on a guy about to jump, threatened to shoot him if he moved. I don't know if the guy jumped or not, but the point is that he was willing to risk that guy's life against some reverse psychology. That's like the thing about, go ahead and do it, who needs you anyway, trying to reverse somebody out of it. Sorry, I don't buy that stuff. What I'm trying to say, maybe somewhere there's something we can find, something I might point out to you that you maybe didn't remember, that you might want to reconsider. I know you're not afraid to die, but maybe this just isn't the time for it. What about your kids? You want them to have to live with the memory of this? What about your friends, is this how you want them to remember you?"

"Bullshit. All I want is out."

"You want out? You can have out. You can have out any time you want, but once you do, you can't ever get back, you ever think of that? I see how you're dressed, how you've got your hair done. It looks quality, it suggests maybe you're pretty good at what it is you do. It suggests you can think, you can handle yourself, you can maybe overcome your problems. Is that a fair reading? Are you maybe shorting yourself out of something?"

She reached a hand back, rubbed it against the texture of the bricks. "I'm just tired of all this. I'm tired of having to be strong, having to cope, having to do it over and over again. I'm just too damn tired to go on. I'm good enough, I'm just too damn tired of it." She turned her head again, to look at him. "You understand that?"

"Lady, we all get tired. That's part of it. You expect everything's gonna be easy, and everything works out in the end just like on TV, but that's not really what life's all about. It mixes good and bad, it's never one thing or another. You got good going for you, you've got to expect some bad to balance it out. You got bad going in your life, there's some good to balance it out, if you'll just notice it. Hell, you're smart, you're good looking, you got all your arms and legs; yeah, lady, your pain is real, but there's others out there would sell their souls for what you've got. Be quality, lady, show me you're a class act. This is just a mistake, you can come back from it, no sweat, you're better than this. Come on, lady, show me you're a class act."

"No, I'm not tough enough to stand this any more. I just can't make it."

There comes a time when it can go either way, whether in a poker game, a love affair, a fist fight, whatever. Lew sensed it was fifty-fifty. "Look," he said, "you're using a permanent solution to a temporary problem. Let's make a deal. I think you're a class act, with enough iron in your spine to make it. I think you've got enough character to win. I'm willing to bet on you, that you're as good as I think you are. If I reach out to you, will you take my hand? I'll be overbalanced, but we can touch. You could jump before I can reach you, you can wait until I get there and then take me with you, or you could help us both get back inside. I'll admit, I'm damn scared to do this, but I see something in you. You won't let me die if I get out there with you, will you? What do you say, will you work with me on this?"

It swung. It swung his way, and he knew it when the light went back on in her soul. The stare was gone, replaced by life. "I ... I'll need help getting back, I'm not sure I can make it."

"Just stay there, stay where you are, and just look at me. I'll help you. Don't move, just stay there. We can make it." He edged out the window, one arm hooked around the window frame.

As he paused for a moment, he felt a hand on his belt. A low voice said, "We all come in, or we all go out, Bro, take your pick."

Then it was easy. His left arm reached out in front of her body, eased her against the wall and slowly drew her to him. They inched back slowly through the window, tense muscles moving in small jumps and twitches. Then it was over, the woman trembling, sobbing, holding him as tight as she could. His arms went tight around her, and he was conscious for the first time of his rapid heartbeat. The Crisis Response Team leader moved closer, his team members with him, to take charge. "Well done, Detective, helluva nice job."

"Yeah, thanks," Lew answered, the adrenaline slowing its rush. "We got two perps downstairs in the unit, Lieutenant, we really got to go in a minute. But hey, look, lady, back in China they say if you save somebody's life, you're responsible for it from then on."

"If that's true," she responded, "then you've inherited one hell of a mess."

"Yeah, maybe, but like I said, I'll bet on you. You'll show me some class, won't you?" He reached into his jacket pocket and came out with a business card. "Here. Things get shitty, you call me, we'll talk about it, all right?"

She took the card, looked at him and said, "Nobody's ever done that for me before."

"Hell, everybody'll do that, you give them half a chance. Look, we got to go. But I meant what I said. You need, you call me."

"I'll do that, Mr., uh, Perkins."

"Lew. And this's my partner, Dan Perkins. Perkins and Perkins, sounds like a law firm, doesn't it? Look, we got to go. You call, huh?" He backed away from her, keeping contact with her hand, until he had to let it go.

As he turned to the door, the next voice began with, "If you'll just come over here, ma'am, we need to …"

"You dig that, Bro?" Dan said, as they passed the eighth floor.

"How the hell do I know, but you've got to admit that would've been one hell of a waste. Good-lookin' woman like that doesn't deserve to be smeared all over the sidewalk. Everybody's got to go some time, but from ten floors up, that's no way. That's bad shit. But, yeah, maybe there's something there. Who the hell knows?" he finished, as they stepped into the lobby.

"I'll tell you something else, who the hell knows, Bro, I knows that you don't know her name. Best hope she don't throw your card away. "

Dan opened the left door and slid into the seat. "Well, we're back, little children, miss us?"

Chapter 3

"CAPTAIN Danilovitch heard about it on the radio. You guys just collected another attaboy. All you need now, is 99 more, you get yourselves a gold star. Unless you get one awshit, which wipes out all your attaboys."

Sergeant Lonnie Marks, 12 days away from retirement, could afford such cynicism. He could afford little else, having an expensive car and two expensive ex-wives to support. "I'm gonna re-marry one of them just in self-defense, soon as I figure out which one's the lesser evil," he'd once said. The thinking around the shift was that he was right. If alimony, as one wag had put it, was the screwing you get for the screwing you got, he might as well get screwed while getting screwed. Of course.

"He also wants to see you, just as soon as you get here. You guys here yet?"

"Yeah, we're here, let us get a couple of minutes to cool down, book our customers here, and then we'll be right in."

"You got it. Just try not to take too long; it's been a bitch of a day, and his temperature's rising."

They walked into the outer office, pausing at the desk just outside the captain's door. As they stood there, they watched Patrolman Horvath C. Swann, his face screwed tight in concentration, one-fingering his way through a long and complicated-looking report on an old manual Remington.

For the last seven months there hadn't been a regular occupant to that chair. They came and they went, just as fast as they could. Swann, in fact, had the best odds to stay, since he was a member of the Rubber Gun Squad. The Rubber Gun Squad consisted of those officers who, by reason of emotional, alcoholic, family or other problems, were deemed "at risk," and relegated to restricted duty. Swann was rumored to be as nutty as a fruitcake and suspected of being among the most intelligent men on the force. He could therefore be faking. Or not. Nobody knew. Nobody cared. Least of all Captain Danilovitch, who now only cared about trying to keep his administrative load no more than three months delinquent, and who, for some reason nobody could fathom, couldn't keep help. At last Swann searched out the last letter in the word he was straining over and looked up.

"Yeah?"

"Captain wants to see us." Dan said.

"Yeah?"

"Yeah," Lew answered.

"In."

"Thanks."

"Yeah. Hey," Swann called after them.

"Yeah?"

"Tell him I'm cured. I'm outa here right now. I either go back on the street tomorrow, or ..." he paused, then made up his mind. "No or. You tell him I'm on the street tomorrow, period."

"Yeah."

* * * * * * * * *

"You wanted to see us, Captain?"

"Yeah. Sit down. Nice job on that jumper dame, glad to see you won. As I recall, you lost one like that before, didn't you?"

"Yessir."

"Well," he mused, "now you're even. Maybe you're a little ahead. People get all wound up in the idea of excitement, major crimes, Mafiosos shooting up the town every hour on the hour, French Connections, they tend to forget that lost kids found and unjumped jumpers are just as important. Nobody gives headlines for CPR-ing some old lady collapsed in a movie house somewhere, or settling domestic disputes, or keeping this city from strangling on its own goddam traffic, or any of that shit, but it's just as important. Well, hell, it all comes with the badge, it's all part of the job. Which is why you're here. Where are you on these serial killings I gave you?"

"Nowhere, Captain, nowhere at all. We caught the latest last night, but there isn't much to go on. Three street punks, three .45

28

caliber shells, no witnesses, no nothing. Best we came up with was some old guy walking his dog, saw the bodies after it happened, called it in. He said he didn't hear anything, so we don't get a good time on it, except for whatever the M.E. can give us on time of death."

Dan added, "It was neat enough for a mob hit, but they generally don't use heavy caliber, and we can't come up with a reason for the mob to want to hit them anyway."

"Shit." Danilovitch leaned back in his chair and spun around to look across the intervening parking lots at the courthouse. "We're gonna catch hell if we don't tie this one up quick, before it gets away from us. Look, I want you to start sliding some of your case load off to other people; get as heavy into this thing as you can. Like I told you before, we're in it up to here if some reporter gets nosey enough to pick this thing up, maybe wants to get his Pulitzer at our expense. And, gentlemen," he heaved his bulk around to glower at them, "if he does, you'll get to be famous. Understood?"

"Yessir, we got it."

"Good. Keep me briefed on all developments; if you need any quiet muscle within the department to expedite anything, you call me. That's all, gentlemen, thank you."

"Okay, Captain. Oh, by the way, one more thing," Lew said. "We got a message for you. Swann, from outside? Says to tell you he's cured, says he's on the street tomorrow."

Danilovitch visibly flinched. "Oh, Goddamn, here we go again. You guys're just pulling my leg. You'd pull shit like this just to get back at me, because I dropped this one on you." His voice turned plaintive. "You are kidding, aren't you? He didn't really bail out, did he?"

"Nope, and yup. Sorry, Captain, we gotta go." Lew said. Dan held a straight face as he moved toward the door. Then he walked out quickly, his face averted from Danilovitch's view. As Lew closed the door, the last thing he heard was Danilovitch saying, "shit!"

As they walked through the corridors of the building known as "Malfunction Junction," Dan's memory replayed their assignment to this running nightmare. They had returned from testifying at the courthouse to find a message slip:

"D. Perkins, L. Perkins — Rpt to Capt Danilovitch Immed upon Rtrn———K. Smith, 0945."

That trip had taken them through an unoccupied outer office, and after knocking and getting a muffled "In," they'd found him sitting behind two stacks of inbound reports and correspondence, running a beefy hand through a rapidly thinning grey crewcut.

Conversational amenities had lasted about three seconds. Then: "Your schedule's pretty light. I made it a point to check. Fact is, you're lighter than anybody else right now, so there's no problem . Plain language, tag, you're it. Aside from your outstanding looks, personalities, talents, luck, and so forth, you're available." He pointed to a stack of case files on one corner of his cluttered desk. "These are yours. You stay with these and with any others that come up and are related, until you get results." With a derogatory flick of his hand he continued, "These are all bad guys, all done within the last few months, all unsolved, obviously, and all apparently unrelated. And all yours. There's now 11 dead bodies, mostly unmourned, seemingly unconnected, that somebody has got to pay for. Even scum like this can't just be offed without due process. What we have here, gentlemen, is what looks like some vigilante; he's going around cleaning up this town. I'm in no mood to argue the social aspects of this; it's illegal, and we're going to stop it. Understood?"

They nodded. "Okay, here's your stack. Get into it and keep me briefed on your progress. This one'll get hot and political quick if it starts to make noise; you know how that goes. Do the usual, do the orthodox, do the unorthodox if need be, but get the answers. Pick this guy up off the streets. Have at it."

And so they'd read the files. Each folder contained all the collected and reported information concerning a different killing, yet each was formatted in the same way. They were as alike as the matched books people buy to fill up their bookshelves, but never get around to reading. Each was enclosed in a tinted manila folder, folded over at the top. These were tinted pink, denoting that they were all homicides. As he'd scanned the first folder, Lew had idly wondered what would happen if they were to discover new crimes that exceeded the number of possible colors. Stripes? Polka dots? Paisleys? For a moment he held a mental picture of a harassed admin sergeant shuffling an in-basket that looked like an interior decorator's nightmare. ("Goddamn, Sergeant, don't you know car theft and computer crime shouldn't go together? They clash!")

The specific layout of each folder was predictable and routinized; upon opening the top cover, you unfolded the sub-cover to the right. That flap contained all the photographs and crime scene sketches, if any, and an envelope for holding the original statements, evidence receipts or other enclosures. Then you lifted the whole stack of papers, all bound at the top with an Acco clip. Each report was laid one on top of the other, with the oldest on the bottom, working upward. The idea behind all this was that the reader could start at the bottom, reading the first report, working his way up to the most current, while able to refer continuously to the right side for the photographs, sketches or whatever, while he read.

Lew had heaved a long sigh, shifted his weight to his elbows, and dug in. Across from him at the facing desk, Dan had reached for half the stack, setting aside all but one. He'd pulled a small tape player from a drawer and put the headphones on. Then he'd leaned way back in his chair, hung his feet on the top desk drawer and started to read.

The silence between them was unbroken except for the sounds of shifting weight back and forth and the slap of tossed files landing on each other's desks. Occasionally they would look up at one another, shrug and return to their reading. After just less than three hours, they'd thrown down the last of the folders.

"Well, what do you think, Lew?"

"I don't. You remember, I told you about that guy I knew, used to get half smashed, then he'd do some of his best thinking? I watched him one night, he worked out a computer problem on a bar napkin, wrapped up a program that'd been bugging him for weeks. He was the same guy, used to get into his car with a problem or something he'd have to think about; he'd let his subconscious take over while he drove. Wound up once or twice in another state, but he'd get the answers he was working on. If there's some kind of serial killer out there, I just don't see it so far. These guys were mostly killed with an array of weapons, in varying kinds of places, at basically different times of day, all kinds of things going down differently. I'm not gonna think. I'm going home. I don't have an answer. I don't want an answer. I want a beer."

Dan rolled his shoulders, getting the kinks out. "Yeah, that's just like you. Basic. You've got your life refined down to just three sentences, you know? Want eat. Want whiskey. Want woman."

"Shows how much you know," Lew said, as he walked toward the door. "You got them in the wrong order, fool."

Chapter 4

IF God doesn't like you, it's pretty hard to get anybody else to like you either. And most definitely, God didn't like Albert Yaschew. God made Albert 5 foot 3, God made Albert weigh 125, and God made Albert's parents name him Albert. It didn't help any that God also made Albert look very much like his father, with thin, receding hair, too much nose, poor eyes and a lack of physical coordination that stopped just mercifully, or unmercifully, short of being handicapped. God could have helped him out a bit, but He didn't.

As near as Albert could figure, it began in the fourth grade, with a teacher. "Albert Yaschew ? What's that? Who's that? Sounds like a sneeze."

The class laughed, and called him, variously, Albert the Sneeze, Albert Sneeze, Albert Snot, anything but what he wanted to be called. Al. ("Call me Al." "Hi, Al." "Hey, come on over, Al." "Hey, there's Big Al." "Yo, Al, how's it goin'?" "My side chooses Al.") Nope, they called him Albert. Aaaaaallllbert. Nobody would have messed with him if his name had been Mike or Rocco, or anything else but Albert. But everybody did. And they'd dare him to do something about it, or even worse, they wouldn't notice when they messed over him. Albert could recount the times when he'd be saying something, and before he could finish a sentence, somebody would interrupt him, changing the subject. Or like, in the cafeteria, he'd try to sit with a group of kids, but as soon as they noticed he was coming, someone would slide their milk and a napkin into the empty place and say "It's saved. Somebody else got here first." He'd know they were lying, but there wasn't anything he could do about it. All through school it had been that way. There was never room for him in a car;

they'd never remember to tell him about parties, girls were always too busy, or they had to wash their hair or something.

And it never got better. Just how great can high school years be, if the high point of your senior year is being selected audio-visual monitor? Albert went stag to the senior prom. So did the homeliest girl in the class, because she'd turned him down. At the graduation ceremonies, the only applause when his name had been called came from his parents. And so it went. God's world didn't like Albert. And Albert cordially returned the favor.

Albert's newspaper lay flat on the kitchen table. He sat on the front edge of the kitchen chair, going through the swiss-cheese-on-white sandwiches.

"The bodies of three gang members were found last night at City Park. Dead are: William David Martin, 19; Lester Arthur Williams, 20; and Francis X. D'Angelo, 19, members of Satan's Sons, a youth gang. All three had been shot, and police theorized that gang rivalries in the area may have motivated the killings, since the three were found with several sharpened screwdrivers, a .22 caliber pistol and homemade blackjacks. A Police Department spokesman stated that several leads were under investigation and arrests were expected shortly. According to Police Department records, these are the 179th, 180th and 181st homicides of the year ..."

Albert grunted with satisfaction. Those kind got what they deserved, they sure had it coming. Just like the clubs in high school that wouldn't let him in ("See, we can only have so many, it's in our constitution, to keep the club from gettin' too big, and we're all full up now.") They were common thugs anyway, muggers, thieves, who-knows what else. Good riddance. Albert carefully clipped the article, and just as carefully taped it into his scrapbook. It just went to show that people who messed over other people, either as criminals or just as insensitive clods, deserved what they got.

Just thinking about it made his blood boil. The whole damn world was unfair, and someday he'd get even with them all. He'd get even. He would; he'd show them what Al Yashew was all about.

When he got to thinking about it this way, he developed enough incentive to put in a little practice. So he went to the bedroom, opened the third drawer of his chest of drawers and removed from under his folded short-sleeved shirts the means by which Al Yashew could show them all. He unwrapped the cloth from the stainless steel .44 magnum, opened the cylinder and dropped six clean, well-polished rounds into his hand. A casual spin of the cylinder, and a sideways flick of the hand to close it, and the gun went into his waistband. In front of the full-length mirror he'd bought for exactly this purpose, he stood, relaxed, watchful, lightning-fast cat reflexes alert. A flashing blur from his right hand, and the heavy gun came up, lined up on the chest of the villain in the mirror, and ... Dah! Dah!, two quick ones, right to the heart. Into the right hip pocket this time, the butt hanging slightly outboard, almost the way John Wayne carried his.

"You feel tough, big bad guy? Try this!" The blur of a hand reaching for the big .44, thumb cocking back the hammer single-action style, ignoring the extra two seconds or so it took to free the snagged front sight from the material of his pocket, the unerring hipshot into the bad guy's leg. "Pow!" A puff of breath down the barrel to clear the smoke, "You still want to try me? Come on. Any time you think you can."

For 20 minutes Albert practiced, visualizing situations. Surrounded by armed muggers, facing down looters on Main Street, coming to the aid of an outnumbered cop, nailing drug kingpins, fast shooting saving the life of an FBI man wounded in the line of duty, and his favorite of all, the lightning draw that convinces one of the Ten Most Wanted to surrender. "You know the position, clown, SUCK WALL!"

Forty-four magnums are big, heavy guns, better suited to killing Buicks than outdrawing bad guys. After those 20 minutes of practice, Albert's hands began to feel the strain, so he flicked the cylinder open again, slamming the cylinder crane against its stop. Six clean cartridges slipped into their chambers, and Albert flicked the gun closed again, in that off-handed swipe that he loved so well. ("Ole Al sure knows his way around guns, don't he? Boy, I sure wouldn't wanna mess with him. Yeah, he should know his way around them. From what I hear, he's got two Silver Stars and a Medal of Honor. Got 'em when he was a Green Beret. Doesn't talk about it much; in fact, he never says anything at all. Quiet guy, sort of like Gary Cooper.")

Big Al laid the gun under his shirts after wiping it down and re-wrapping it in the soft white flannel square. The minor damage to the cylinder latch and crane from the repeated flicking and slamming never came to his attention. Anyway, the minor distortions and the hairline crack wouldn't have shown, even if he'd known where to look. Big Al turned out the light and walked back into the living room, just in time for another cop show.

* * * * * * * * *

In the quiet hours of the evening, after the oldest and most feeble residents had gone to bed, they gathered in the dayroom. A few arranged themselves in the overstuffed chairs, finding little comfort for their arthritic joints in any position. Those most able to sat in the institutional stackable plastic chairs arranged around the several card tables. The low murmur of talk drifted through the room, a mixture of complaints over illnesses real and imagined, anecdotes about grandchildren and great-grandchildren, mixed with the rustling of newspapers and the unending sighs and coughs.

"I guess we're all here, so we might as well call this meeting to order," Howard Kirk said softly. "Since I was the last number up, I'll just report, and then we'll move on to new business. I operated in the park, where that gang runs — used to run. They tried to mug me for my money — tried the same thing on me that they did on poor Floyd Regensburg. I got all three who tried." He was interrupted by a voice at his side. "Yeah, that was what they wanted, but they sure got something else, I can tell you."

Howard turned. "How'd it look to you, Charlie?" Charlie McMorriss smiled and patted the dog in his lap. "It looked very good, Howard," he said. "They were all laid out cool as a cucumber, they were, nary so much as a twitch. Didn't see another soul after you walked off, and that hollow sure muffled the sounds. Say, maybe I didn't put on a good act for those young cops, too, let me tell you. Smooth as silk," he chortled, "the way I can string 'em together. Say, maybe I ought to run for Congress, or sell used cars." He grew thoughtful for a moment, and continued. "But maybe it isn't such a good idea for us to call the police, too. Being there's one thing, but maybe a low profile'd be better. They've got my name now, and that sort of worries me a little bit."

"All right," Howard answered, "fair enough." I guess nobody saw me, and I got away clean, but I do have to tell you, I had an awful scare when my heart started acting up. I wasn't sure I'd make it back here. All in all, though, I think we can say it went very well."

"Yah, you see?" a voice piped up from the back row, "I told you and I told you, but you wouldn't listen. You can't go out there alone. You need somebody with you. You need backup, just like on them cop shows."

"All right, Tom, point well taken, we'll try it your way." Howard's faded blues eyes scanned the group. "If there're no objections, we'll try working in twos , maybe even threes if it seems all right with each action member. But I think we ought to make that a matter of individual choice." No one spoke, so he continued: "We'll hear from the Selection Committee now, please."

Martha Hamilton stood up, adjusted her bifocals, cleared her throat, and with a theatrical flourish opened a folded sheet of paper. "The Selection Committee proposes," she paused for effect: "Arthur Pierce Fitzgerald, age 32, last tried for drug trafficking, acquitted by the bench following suppression of evidence, based upon the illegality of a search and seizure. He has 25 arrests, four previous convictions, did three years for armed robbery, did one for aggravated assault with a baseball bat. And just before his last arrest, he walked on a rape charge when the victim withdrew her testimony against him. Pretty obvious somebody got to her. A thoroughly bad apple, and a perfect candidate for the Action Committee. After watching him in court for three days, I'd like to take him myself. Smirking pup, I'd take some starch out of him, you can bet."

"Now, Martha," Howard chided, "we've been through this before. If you're on the Selection Committee, you can't be part of the Action Committee. It's just not good organization. Of course, you're free to drop out of Selection if you like, but you do such good work and you understand everything that's going on at the courthouse; I don't know if we'd get as good results as you get, without you. But it's your choice, either way you like."

"No, " she conceded, "I'm just mad at this young whippersnapper, thinks he's got the world by the tail and nothing'll ever happen to him. I just want to nominate him real good."

Howard straightened up and in a firm voice said, "The Chair will entertain a motion for the nomination of Arthur Pierce, uh, Fitzgerald, for removal. Do I hear a motion?"

"So made."

"Thank you, Charlie; now, is there a second?" Several hands went up. "All those in favor?" A general raising of hands. "All those opposed?" A pause. "Motion carries, the Planning Committee will take it from here. The next order of business is the Planning Committee. Beatrice?"

Bea Haggerty shifted her substantial bulk out of a sprung-bottomed old Morris chair and smoothed her dress over her ample thighs. "Our subject for planning at the last meeting was Tonio Macario, who was nominated last month. I'm sorry it took so long, but he moved and we had to find him again. According to the routine we worked up on him, the best time seems to be late in the afternoon, when he's working at that wrecking yard on the west side. Later at night he's either with a lot of people, or he's in areas we can't get into. We recommend taking him in that auto parts place. There're three entrances, so we should be able to get in and out real easy. We just don't know what to use. It's pretty well populated. Thought we'd leave that up to you, Howard."

One of the other residents griped, "So who's he, Georgie Patton? How come he gets to run this thing and pick and choose, like this was his own private party? Who made him boss anyway?"

"We did, Walter, you old fool," chirped another. "Now you just hush up and let the meeting continue. Go ahead, Howard."

Howard's hand unconsciously strayed to the Silver Star medal he carried in his pocket, its contours long worn smooth. "I'm just up here because of my previous experience, Walter, but I don't mind stepping down, if that's what the group wants. We're doing this the democratic way, after all. But until somebody calls for a vote," his voice took on a hard edge, "I'd appreciate it if you'd stop trying to undercut me. Now, I'd like to get on with this, if you don't mind. I'm tired and it's getting late." He turned and said, "Beatrice, if you'll accept my recommendation, I think a .22 caliber rifle'd work pretty well. We've got one that uses magnums, and we can put a silencer and a telescopic sight on it, so it wouldn't even have to be a hard shot."

"Thank you, Howard," she answered, "that sounds just fine to me, if it's acceptable to the Action Committee." She sat down and picked up a piece of embroidery work, delicately running the needle through the outline of a rose.

"Next order of business," Howard said, moving ahead, "is the Action Committee. We'll take two this time, Charlotte, if you please."

Charlotte Heatherly blushed at having to come to the front of the group. She'd always been painfully shy and had limited her social life accordingly. In fact, she had earned a family nickname, "Poor Charlotte," and was always called that when spoken about by relatives. Her mousiness had long become part of the family's lore. She was the maiden aunt who ate in the kitchen and watched from behind the window curtains as life went by. Still painfully shy, she crept up to the front of the room holding a shoebox in her hand. Poor Charlotte held the shoebox over the head of first one and then another resident, then handed the pieces of paper drawn by their hands to Howard.

Howard read the papers, then spoke: "Herman Burgess and Ellie Florissant, if that's all right with you."

Herman rose and addressed the room. "I've already been out on one, so I'm not sure I can legally go out on another one when others haven't had their turn, but if nobody has any objections, I'd like to take this one, too."

Ellie spoke up: "It's fine with me, Herman, I've done one before, too, and I think I'd do even better on this one. After all, experience always helps. The more you do, the better you get. Bang, bang, it's all over, and we've cleaned up another piece of garbage." She grinned, "I'll even match you for the shot. We'll practice together."

"Yeah, I can guess what they'll be practicing," Hubert Graves snickered. "Hey, Herman, you knock her up, you gotta marry her, y'know."

The room dissolved in laughter as Howard called several times for order. "All right, folks, let's please settle down and finish the meeting. Is there any other new business?"

A voice from the back of the room caught his attention. "Yeah, Howard, there is one thing I'd like to put before the Planning Committee, or maybe just throw it out for general consideration. We're running low on ammunition, what with everybody wanting to go downstairs and practice all the time. We need to either start rationing it, or else we need to set up some trips to somewhere to buy some more. We just can't afford to let everybody use all they want, any time they want."

Howard looked around the room. "Comments?" he asked. "If not, I'll have to agree with Davey on this, and I'd like to select a committee to handle it. Burt, how about you taking it, getting a couple of others to work with you, and come up with some proposed solutions, say, in time for our next meeting?" As Burt nodded, he continued, "If there isn't any other new business, I'll entertain a motion to adjourn this meeting. Is there a motion?"

"Iseeamotionisthereasecondallinfavorsayaye,opposednay,theayes haveitmeeting'sadjourned." He dragged in a full breath. "That said, Herman, Ellie, let's get together tomorrow and work out the details, we'll fix up the rifle, and you can get your practice in. Good night, folks, these old bones just went beddy-bye."

As the members filed out, the noise level dropped off until the silence was broken only by a late movie on the television set. There in front Charlie McMorriss sat, absently scratching behind Sugar's ear. In a chair behind him, Tom Euberhold lay slouched in a chair, softly snoring.

Chapter 5

DAVEY Grimes enjoyed a unique position within the city's police department. In his second year on the force, he'd come to the favorable attention of a very sharp captain who had already been picked for bigger things. He'd come to that captain's attention by the simple expedient of busting in on a bad situation in a downtown bank and removing said captain's wife from a hostage situation with a large dose of street smarts and two well-placed bullets. By the time notified units had arrived, Davey's well-developing skills as a cop and his incredible luck to have needed to make a mortgage payment on his day off had bonded his career permanently to that of a police captain who loved his wife.

In the military, the process is known as hitching one's wagon to a rising star. In the world of business, it's called having a mentor, or a sponsor. In most police departments, it's called having a rabbi. And from that moment on, young Davey had a rabbi. Young Davey's rabbi made sure he got rotated through as many squad assignments as possible. Developing Davey's rabbi made sure he got assigned to as many training schools, including the FBI school at Quantico, as possible. Mature Davey's rabbi made sure he was able to get his degree in time to have it count toward the selection board's recommendations for Lieutenant. And when Davey's rabbi made Chief, Davey was selected to run a small elite unit whose purpose was to provide administrative, tactical, training and whatever other assistance they could to the rest of the department. Organizationally, they stood something halfway between the academy and Internal Affairs; their charter was to "help the screwed-up — individuals, units, whoever — on the streets, at their desks, wherever."

A nice job. A good career move. An excellent chance to prove out if you were Chief material. And a good place from which to perpetuate the rabbi system. Lieutenant, soon to be Captain on the next selection board, Davey Grimes was Lew's rabbi.

Davey made sure the right people knew who Lew was. Davey made sure Lew became a member of the Holy Name Society, an officer in the Police Benevolent Association, a known cop. Most times, Lew had to fend for himself. Having a rabbi wasn't a guarantee, as many a marginal cop found out. If you're not any good, you make your rabbi look bad. Sometimes you can get away with it, but most times you don't. So when Lew walked in on Davey Grimes, the odds were it had to be either a social call or a very troublesome professional dilemma.

"I've been through these freakin' reports so many times, Lieutenant, I'm wearing out the ink. I don't see it. I get bupkis. Zip. Nada. Nothing, no way, no how. There's ungatz in these. No connections, no acquaintances, no similarities, no relatives cross-connected, no joint jobs, no records, nobody went to prison together, nothing. I'm desperate for a new idea. I can't find the common thread that ties them together."

"Okay, let me take a look. Maybe there's something there that requires a keener intellect than yours. Hell, anybody's got a keener intellect than yours, you dumb-ass hillbilly. You've got the IQ of a tree stump."

Lieutenant Davey Grimes carefully shifted his sore left leg and mentally cursed for the thousandth time the new class of rookies who'd just graduated from the academy. As an afterthought he added a few curses in his own direction, for having walked around the back of a rookie-driven unit without thumping on the fender, yelling, shooting flares, generally doing whatever the hell it would take to let the rook know not to back up.

"Yeah, but at least I'm smart enough not to let some rookie put tire tracks across my ass." Lew's grin faded. "Seriously, I'd appreciate any kind of insight you can offer on this one. It's a bitch, the Captain's going crazy, and we're no closer than we were on day one. If you've got the time, I'd sure like your help."

Grimes' hand curled around the stack. "Well, I'm not pulling full duty yet, so let me see what I can come up with. Now get the hell out of here before I tell everybody in the house that the great Perkinses are stuck for an idea."

* * * * * * * * * *

Nobody works all the time. At least you try not to, even if you're a cop. This Friday night was one of those nights Lew didn't want to be home, drowning in the quiet. He'd had enough of that since the divorce, and the time was long over when he felt justified in moping and feeling sorry for himself. So this wasn't a night to stay home and brood. It was a night to get the hell out, which is exactly what he did.

He remembered a bar he'd been to a long time ago, on the south side of town. He'd originally been there on business, chasing down a hot check artist, and had liked the atmosphere. It seemed to cater to a slightly older crowd, which was just fine with him. This night he felt like a hundred, and there just wasn't any interest in fending off some young honey whose IQ equaled her bust size, and who equated carrying a gun with some sort of macho thing.

As he aimed the Great White Whale toward Crawford's, he remembered the case that had brought him there the first time. It had been a piece of cake. He'd recalled that an instructor at the academy had mentioned to him over a beer one time, that although the majority of hot check artists would go to great lengths to obtain varying ID and change their appearances and even their handwriting, they almost never consider changing the way they write the basics of the check. Dates, numerical expressions, placement of words, these consistently follow a particular style. Lew laughed out loud, remembering how he caught up with his perp. The poor clown hadn't ever varied from writing "rd" after the date, as in "March 24rd," and consistently wrote the words, "Dollards and None Cents" on every check he passed, every time.

Lew came back to the real world as he turned in off the street. He parked at the end of a row, narrowing the driveway by half, locked the door and walked inside.

Once inside, he turned left and walked up the two steps to the bar level. The bar was roughly 30 or so feet long, curved and comfortably dim. He walked along it looking for a seat, found one and sat down, simultaneously asking the woman next to it, "This one an empty?"

She looked up at his reflection on the back bar mirror and waved her hand. He ordered a beer and scanned the mirror, becoming aware of the atmosphere and the postures of the other occupants at tables around the dance floor, sensing whether he could be a civilian relaxing or about to become a cop again. The mood seemed easy, the feel was right, so he allowed himself to relax another notch.

A voice broke into his consciousness, saying, "You owe the lady for my beer."

"Huh?"

"I said, you owe the lady for my beer. I looked it up, and you were right. In China, when you save somebody's life, you're responsible for them. So pay my bar tab."

"Huh?"

She made a face. "You're a brilliant conversationalist, Perkins, you know that?"

"Uh, well, I ..." Then he recognized the face. "Oh, hell, yes, I'm sorry, I just wasn't thinking too clearly there for a second. How're you doing?"

"Pretty good. No, real good. Did you know attempted suicide's a misdemeanor? Costs you a hundred bucks, plus court costs. Also a bunch of therapy, which I guess I really needed." She looked him directly in the eye and held his gaze. "You know," she said, "you really did a brave thing that day, pulling me back in. You could've let me die, and you didn't. I'm terribly grateful for that."

"Well," Lew answered, "it scared the hell out of me, too, but as long as it came out all right," he shrugged, "no harm done. Sometimes things balance out. It sort of makes up for the dirty end of the job." He turned full to her again and asked, "You're really doing all right? Hey, I'm sorry, but I never got your name. What is it?"

She held out a hand to him. "Mary Catherine O'Hara. My friends call me Mary Kate. You're a friend."

He took her hand and felt the warm strength in it. Her grip was firm. "Lew Perkins. You got good hands, Mary Kate. You gonna keep 'em alive?"

"You can bet the farm on it, Lew. The therapy helped a bunch and there's a support group, but the real biggie came from you. You

44

said you wanted me to show you I was a class act, you remember that? Well, it struck a nerve, pretty deep down. All the years with that bum changed my perception of myself, and you brought it all back with that one well-turned phrase. Class act. You ever think of being a poet, you could use that one. Anyway, I was brought up as a class act, even through some bad times. That's what I was before, it's what I am, and it's what I'll always be. That episode put everything back into focus for me." She cocked her head, listening for a moment to the music the band was playing, then slid off the stool. "Come dance with me, Perkins."

"Yeah, that's slow enough, I can handle that without falling over. See, I'm really not much of a dancer."

"That's okay, neither am I, but I learned anything's worth a try."

Lew eased off the bar stool, noticed with some surprise that she was almost as tall as he. "Lead on, lady. I'll try anything once. Or twice. Or three times; maybe even ..."

"Shut up and dance."

The evening wasn't nearly long enough. Lew had started holding her at what he'd interpreted as a socially acceptable distance and had ended up with her head on his shoulder, the vague perfume of her hair in his nostrils. The talk and the beer opened them to one another, and Lew liked what he found. Very much.

As they reclaimed their seats for the last time, she placed her hand on his arm, looking directly into his eyes in a mannerism he found seemed to explain her whole personality. "Look, Lew, I don't know where all this is going, but wherever it goes, I think that's all right with me."

"Lady, I was hoping you'd say that. I want to get to know you a whole lot better. Look, I'm not a real warm personality. My ex used to say there wasn't a lot of love in me. I won't offer you love. I can't offer you love. But right now, I can offer you a pretty strong case of like."

She took his hand between both of hers. "You got a deal, friend."

* * * * * * * * * *

It wasn't Holden's fault that the lousy cops had arrested him again. When he knocked the old woman down and took her purse, the lousy cops drove right around the corner and damn near ran

45

him down where he stood, with the purse in his hand. It sucked. It really did, the whole hassle of being picked up, handcuffed, pushed into the lousy cop car, being driven to the lousy police station, the same stupid questions, the dumb fingerprint shit, the stupid thing with the mug photos, just all that booking hassle. It sucked.

And what made it all the more stupid was the fact that Holden would just sit in the chair, just like all the other times, gaze up at the ceiling while some stupid, lousy cop tried to ask him questions, just like the other time, and then when the stupid lousy cop ran out of breath, Holden would tell the ceiling, just like the other times, "I decline to make any statement without the benefit of counsel present. I request to call my lawyer immediately. I decline to any statement without ..." Eventually, the stupid lousy cop would get the idea, and Holden would then call his father's lawyer, and the lawyer would come down, make the stupid, lousy cops let him go, and then later talk to some judge and get it all thrown out of court. Stupid hassles, they sucked.

This time around, the stupid, lousy cops had been really pissed. They were mad, man, because when they looked up his record, they found that his father's lawyer had gotten the last case thrown out of court just three weeks ago. That was the one where the stupid damn old lady hit her head on the street when she fell and fractured her skull. His old man got mad, just like all the other times, and his old lady cried, just like all the other times.

This last time things seemed to work a lot slower. The stupid lousy cops took their time booking him; then they told him the stupid, lousy phone was busy, denying him the use of his own cell phone, and he had to wait. So they made him sit in a stupid, lousy cell, with a bunch of low-life criminals. By the time they let him make his phone call, Holden was really pissed. Who the hell did they think they were messing with? He tried to tell the stupid, lousy cop what a mistake he was making, but couldn't get anywhere. And it was forever, man, before the stupid, lousy lawyer got there.

"I swear, this is the last time. You either straighten up or your ass goes into the Army. When I was your age ..." Holden knew the speech by heart. So he stared up at the cathedral ceiling in the family room, which his father liked to call "the great room." Holden didn't know why, it was just stupid shit that real estate developers

46

like his father just did, and Holden nodded at the appropriate places while he waited for his mother to interject her themes. There were three. There was, "I don't know what to do about you"; there was, "We have a certain standing in this community," and there was, "How can I hold my head up at the Club?" It varied which came first, but they were always there.

They were the same themes he'd heard ever since he was 12 years old, the year he'd set that cat on fire. After a while he got tired of hearing the same old shit. So he got up out of his chair, went to his room, got his car keys and walked out. All the while his old man and his old lady kept up their stupid goddamn yapping. It wasn't until the front door closed on his father's last "where the hell do you think you're going?" that he unwound a little. With the stereo turned up in the red Firebird, he cruised slowly east, heading the few miles into the midtown area.

Over near the old folks' home, the one where he'd spotted the old lady who walked around the block all the time. Just thinking about it started the rush. He remembered the first time, how he'd staked her out. It was so cool, so cool, man, how he did it. After he saw her, he pulled the 'bird around the corner and parked down the block. Then he jumped out and walked past her. Then, man, the neat part, he ran almost all the way around the block, crossed the street, and stalked her all the way back to that old folks' home. For the next couple of nights he repeated the same thing. Got so, he knew by what time it was where he'd find her.

This was the night, man, this was her turn. He needed to relax some, and the best way he knew was to take down that old bitch. One quick one, dump her on her ass, get the purse, then split. Get a little money, go hang out somewhere, have some fun.

Holden checked the intersection, then pulled over to the far curb and sat. He was a few minutes early, so he waited. Quietly now, anticipating how it would be. He decided to get mellow. Not a lot, just a small hit, so he reached down under the front seat and pulled out his father's briefcase which he'd lifted for this specific purpose about three months ago. He unzipped the soft, heavily waxed Gucci leather and felt among his father's missing papers, leases, business cards and all that shit, and pulled out the baggie containing his stash. All pre-rolled mechanicals, they were carefully made. Nothing but the best for Holden. Goddamn, but that was a stupid, lousy name to hang on somebody. His stupid father named him after that asshole in "Catcher in the Rye." Stupid goddamn book anyway. Who gave a shit about some kid growing up way back then? Didn't matter anyway, nothing mattered.

Just as he was about to light the cigarette, Holden's gaze lit on the old lady. Sure as hell, there she was, holding a big-assed purse by the straps. He watched as she walked the length of the block, then eased out of the car as she turned the corner. With her back to him there wasn't any risk of her seeing the dome light. Not that anybody'd care, not around here anyway. Shitty neighborhood, midtown, who gives a rat's?

Holden sprinted to the corner on expensively silent designer sneakers and cautiously looked around the building's corner. There she was, walking in the middle of the sidewalk, just about to go into a tunnel-like growth of trees. He took a couple of deep breaths to fill his lungs with oxygen and started to run. As he ran, the padding of his sneakers was barely audible, although it didn't really matter. Even with all the warning in the world, no old lady was going to give him a hard time. As he drew closer, he started to reach for her purse, grabbed hold of it and got ready to give a sharp yank. Except that he didn't have to. The old lady picked that moment to fall down, and he got away with the purse clean. As Holden took the next two steps, he caught a dark vision of a man-shaped thing, coming out of the trees to his left, holding something over his shoulder. Like a bat, maybe a club, maybe, OHJEEZUZGOD, a big freakin' knife, a sword, some shit .... and Holden passed the man, still at a dead run, suddenly realizing that, whatever thing the man had held, he missed. Holden kept running another 20 feet or so, feeling good, but conscious that he was growing tired. Maybe too much of a run, damn near two full sides of the block. Too much run. Have to watch that next time.

As the fatigue caught up with him, he slowed, then stopped. The bag began to weigh heavily in his hands, more than before. He leaned over and put his hands on his knees to rest for just a minute, before running on. Besides, it was hot out and his shirt was wet with sweat, dripping down onto the sidewalk. It was funny-looking sweat, Holden thought, there was a lot of it, and it was dark. Almost as dark as the night was getting, as his vision narrowed to a small area at his feet. He felt tired, more tired than he'd ever been before. And sleepy. Too sleepy to run on, Holden let his legs flex so that he could lay down for just a second, to get a little sleep.

Elsa Van Damm straightened up, softly calling to the shadows, "Is that it?" The shadows answered back, "It is done. Go home now, quickly." In the darkness there was a metallic slithering sound and a soft click, almost too soft to hear, as an ancient sword returned to its scabbard.

As Elsa's footsteps faded into the night, Sunihiro Saito, his entire body swathed in black, stepped softly with padded feet to where Holden lay. He paused to make sure there was no more blood spurting from the artery he'd severed. Then, without a sound, he picked up the purse and melted back into the shadows of the trees.

Several minutes later an owl, looking for its dinner, noticed the soft flowing movements in the shadows on a heavily treed street. It observed for a moment, then rejected its vision as possible food, since it appeared to be too large to attack. It wheeled, moved further along the line of bushes and trees, then dived soundlessly on a mouse.

Chapter 6

THERE are certain things you do and don't do, if you have a gun, depending upon who you are. If you're a criminal, you carry it wherever you please, use it whenever you want to, however you want to, and you don't worry about little things like licenses. After all, if you're antisocial enough to commit armed robbery, or even murder, what's a little license violation? It's like being a bank robber, but never parking your getaway car in a no-parking zone. On the other hand, if you're a reasonably law-abiding type, and you happen to own an unlicensed gun, you hide it away, never take it outside and never, never use it. Because, even if you use it to save your own life or maybe someone else's life, in this city they'll arrest you for owning an unlicensed weapon. No matter that you've just blown away some homicidal maniac about to kill Mother Theresa or even the mayor, they'll bust you. No medal, just 30 days.

Which is why Albert never used to take his gun out with him. He obeyed the laws of man. Then he decided to obey the laws of God. It was hard for him to come to the proper conclusion; in fact, it took five coin tosses before God gave him a sign that it was all right to go out with the gun hidden under his jacket. And it felt good. He'd walked halfway down Main, crossed over, walked past his block, crossed again, and nobody'd bothered him. Not one bit. Even better, he'd walked past several obvious street thugs, dressed grubbily in paint-spattered jackets, who'd probably have liked to jump him, but didn't. Maybe it was the confidence in the way he walked or the cool steel in his eyes, or maybe they'd seen and recognized the shape of the bulge under his jacket. Either way, they'd been too afraid to mess with Big Al Yaschew, that was for sure.

So on another night he did it again. This time he walked to the small mom-and-pop grocery, got some sliced Swiss cheese, some white bread and some V-8 (you could live forever on those three) and walked home feeling stronger, taller, baaaaadder than ever before. No doubt about it, had an armed robber dropped in on their grocery store, Big Al would've been a real surprise.

("Who are you anyway, Mister?"

"Depending on who YOU are, I'm either the Seventh Cavalry or your worst nightmare.")

And so it went. By deep autumn, Al routinely carried the gun, now almost wishing something could happen to validate his hours of quick-draw practice and to lend substance to all the routines he'd talked himself through in the mirror. At night, Big Al walked, no, PATROLLED the streets of his neighborhood, daring something to happen. Now it was a comfortable routine. The .44 magnum slipped into his belt, he'd go shopping, eyes careful to check every doorway, every stranger, classifying them as citizens or hoods. He'd carry home his bag of groceries (left arm only, thank you, keeps the right free to draw) and watch a little TV. He'd get in a little practice, and then after the ten o'clock news was over, he'd check the loads, flicking the cylinder shut in the motion he loved so well, pack his iron, put on his jacket and walk, full of confidence, to the little bar on Main. There Big Al would sit quietly, unbothered by the crowd, but ever watchful, ever alert. The fact that no one spoke to him he chalked up to the steely dangerousness in his eyes. It never dawned upon him that his appearance was so unassuming, so unnoticeable, that people barely recognized his presence. No. He was just too bad to mess with.

On that Friday night he finished his third beer at the usual twelve-thirty, straightened his jacket and walked out the door. He turned south, away from his apartment house, to get a little more walking in. After two blocks he turned around again. And it came to pass that Big Al Yaschew was 20 feet away from the door of the Midtowner Lounge when two shots cracked the night, and he was 15 feet from the door when the two armed men backed out, and he was ten feet from them when they turned in his direction.

And Big Al was ready, Big Al was trained, Big Al did what he'd practiced, without thinking about it. Left hand pulled the zipper down; right hand flashed in, came out with the heavy .44. His normally high-pitched voice rose to soprano as he shouted, "Freeze, asshole!" And in less than five seconds, it was all over. Robber Number One raised his gun. Al's first shot drilled him right through the breastbone.

And the hairline crack in the latch of Al's gun gave way. The cylinder fell out to the left, just as Al's panicked brain realized what he'd done; he'd actually shot somebody, maybe killed him. And as he tried to make his leaden left hand close the gun, knowing that now he needed it more than ever, Robber Number Two emptied three .38 caliber slugs into Al, throwing him backward onto the cracked sidewalk.

Albert lay spread-eagled under the sodium-vapor street light, watching it grow dim. The gun lay between his knees, like some disjointed phallic symbol that mocked what he'd wanted to become. On the night before his 28th birthday, Albert Morton Yaschew saw the light go out and recognized the theme of his life in the sound of footsteps leaving him behind.

* * * * * * * * * *

The call came at 1:17. It rescued him from a nightmare, one in which he was being pursued by some destructive machine that wanted to chew him up. The switch to turn it off was hanging out in front of him, and however fast he ran, the switch stayed just out of reach. In the time it took for him to find the phone, he had lost the thought of the dream.

"Hello?"

"Lew." It was Dan. "Get dressed, Bro, we got another one."

"Huh?"

"Wake up, asshole! Slap whoever it is on the ass, tell her to go home, and get your pants on. We gotta go to work, my man, they're playing our song. You conscious yet?"

"Yeah, yeah, I'm awake," Lew grumped, "and there's nobody to slap on the ass. Awright, I'm up; where is it, how come it's ours, and what's been done so far?"

She was looking at him as he turned on the light and started to dress.

"You heard?"

"Yeah, particularly that part about nobody to slap on the ass. Since when am I a nobody?"

He grinned. "Just maintaining your cover, lady. Class acts like you don't hit the sheets with street cops like me."

"The hell they don't," she said. "You're the best thing's happened to me since I don't know when. You, I don't throw back." She rolled out his side of the bed, turned past him and reached for a tie from his open closet door. "Here, this goes with that jacket, not that horrible rag you've got there.

"Don't like my clothes, huh?"

"Buster, " she said, "what I like about you ain't your clothes."

When he finished dressing, he reached for his holstered gun on the dresser. As he did, the expression on her face changed. He looked, read the same message he'd read too many times before. "Sorry," he said, as he snapped the clip over his belt, "but it comes with the job. Remember what I said, about you got to take the good and the bad together?"

As he pulled on his coat, she climbed back onto the bed, kneeling at the side of the mattress and tugging down the tails of the shirt she'd appropriated from him. "Good and bad, huh? Well, the bad news is, you've got six hours to get back here before I get up and leave. The good news is, if you're not back on time, I'll be back tonight."

Suddenly she sobered and jumped back off the bed, to stand close in front of him. Her hand traced his cheekbone as her eyes tried to read his. "All of a sudden, I think I understand. You'll be careful, won't you?"

Lew smiled down at her. "Lady, I'm always careful. I never take a risk I don't have to."

"You did for me, Lew."

"I had to do that," he said. "I couldn't let you go out like that. Damn glad, too." She laid her cheek against his shoulder for a moment. As he turned at his apartment door, she was still standing there watching him.

Lew arrived in the Great White Whale, as he called his old Oldsmobile. Since it looked all right, ran beautifully and came equipped with Lew's version of mobile crime lab and machinist's shop, with room left over for his golf bag and shoes, he saw no reason to give it up. Besides, it was paid for, which made it damn well beautiful. He eased in to some unused space at the curb, getting out just as Dan approached.

"I'm here just a couple of minutes before you, Bro, but I think I'm gonna like this day, no matter when it started. This here used to be Charles Hartley, male cauc, 26, genuine bad-ass, now retired. No great loss. But the other one, stud, get this, is Albert M. Yaschew, who we ain't never heard of before. And this Yaschew's got himself a Dirty Harry gun, with one slug gone. I give you one guess where the slug's at. Now let's not get all hot 'n' wet 'n' slippery over this, but ..." he took a long breath, "isn't it interesting that there's this here bad guy dead, from this here good guy? It sure suggests we got ourselves one dead vigilante-type killer."

Lew eyeballed the general scene for a moment. "Do we know yet what happened, Dan?"

"From the witnesses we get in the bar, there was two yahoos dropped in to hold the place up, maybe 10, 15 minutes after this little guy left. He's sort of a regular, comes in, has two, three beers, never says anything to anybody. Generally leaves a little after midnight; nobody knows much about him. This other guy here, he and his partner had themselves a small payday, put two rounds into the ceiling on the way out. From what the people in the bar say, it almost looks like the little guy here ambushed them coming out, and they got into a regular shootout. Nobody seems to know where the gun came from. Guess it had to be the little guy's. Anyway, the M.E. suggests the little guy did Hartley, but Hartley didn't do the little guy. Hartley's piece has four rounds left in it, and all the witnesses agree he put two into the ceiling. A regular Dillinger, this clown. Dumbshit. We also got a partial description of Hartley's buddy. It's going out right now."

Lew carefully picked up the .44 magnum, then glanced down, and concentrated on the chalked outline where the gun had lain. "I wonder what it is makes people, for some reason, want to go out and buy cannons like this? Way too much gun, unless you got hands like a gorilla and arms to match. Who the hell needs a gun like this? You can't hit shit from more than 20 feet, and for a little guy like this, the recoil's uncontrollable. Well, what the hell, his choice, I guess."

"It's busted," Dan observed, "the cylinder latch is broken. It won't close. Poor little guy got screwed by whoever'd sell him a busted gun."

Lew pulled a cigarette from the crushed pack in his pocket, thumbed a light from his dilapidated Zippo he insisted on carrying instead of a disposable butane lighter. As he cleared his mind, he focused on the lighter itself. It was getting tougher to find lighter fluid these days, and he knew he'd eventually have to retire it, but he held onto it, half out of curiosity to see how long it would last and half because of the engraving on it. He'd had it done in Vietnam, when he'd been young and strong and believed in his own immortality. Now he wasn't too sure any more, but he still liked the parody of the 23rd Psalm engraved on his old Zippo:

"Yea, though I walk through the valley of the shadow of death, I will fear no evil, for I am the evillest mother in the valley."

He returned his attention to Dan and said, "Dan, what makes us think this's our guy? We got .38's, we got .45's, we got one knifing, we got maybe even a hit-and-run that could be one of ours. With no particular consistency to the M.O., how do we figure this," he pointed with his foot, "this's our vigilante?"

"We don't, Bro, not yet, but it starts to look good. Look, let's do our thing here, grab some breakfast, then we'll follow this Yaschew back a couple of years. See where he came from, see maybe does he have a sheet somewhere. It's thin, yeah, but we got nothing better to do anyway, do we?" "Yeah," Lew mumbled, "we got nothing better to do."

Chapter 7

THE building Albert Yaschew had lived in was one of those old, three-story brick monstrosities with the fake Grecian columns along the front porch. Along the three sides of the porch and two stories up was the tesselated woodwork that passed for artistic embellishment in those days. They went in through a screen door whose weight was doubled by layers of chalking white paint and checked the mailboxes on the wall. In blue plastic Dymo label tape they found the "A. Yaschew" they were looking for, over 303. They also found "J. Carter" and the word "Manger" over apartment 101. Lew poked his partner and softly said, "J. Carter, huh?"

"Do you suppose ... naw, probably not."

Dan picked up on it. "Hey, man, could be, after all, you think what he was like, then you read here on the tape where it says, 'Manger.' Hell, it's possible, anybody else'd have said 'Manager.' On second thought, naw, he's got that farm and all down where it's warm, what the hell would he want a part-time job up here for?"

Lew deadpanned, "You're right, couldn't possibly be him. Let's ring the manger bell; see if we get ex-presidents, cows or what."

The bell didn't work, which didn't particularly surprise either of them. At the third knock the door opened, revealing a gentleman who was decidedly not HIM, and who said, "Help you?"

Dan lifted the folder containing his picture ID card and badge from his coat pocket and held it up at approximately eye level. "My name is Perkins, sir, Dan Perkins. This's my partner, Lew Perkins. As you can guess," he said, with measured gravity, "we're not really related. But what we are is, we're police officers, and we'd appreciate your assistance and cooperation in a matter presently under investigation, if you can spare a few minutes."

"Huh?"

Dan tried again. "Cops, Bro, no bust, but we need to talk, you dig?"

"Oh, yeah," said J. Carter, "Okay, nothing to hide anyway, what's it about? Come in, come on in." He held the door open, letting them into the living room.

A worn overstuffed couch faced the console TV set. The coffee table in front of it held a stack of newspapers and magazines and a worn leather Bible. A cat sitting on the back of the sofa looked up without curiosity at the two cops, then resumed watching the program on the screen. Chairs filled out the corners of the room, and several pictures on the mantle over the long unused fireplace lent an air of family and home to the room. The pictures showed a chronology from a smiling black soldier in his early 20s, through a black couple, progressively older, with several faded prints of black teenagers, all wearing caps and gowns, in traditional poses. Dan's glance from left to right across the mantle told him how this interview would go. "We're conducting an investigation, sir, involving one of your tenants. You have an Albert M. Yaschew?"

"Oh, my, yes," Carter said. "He's in 303, upstairs. He done anything? He don't seem the sort for trouble, him being quiet and all. What'd he do?"

"He didn't do anything, sir. As a matter of fact, I'm sorry to have to tell you that he was killed early this morning, in front of the Midtowner Lounge out on Main. He was shot, I'm afraid." Dan let that sink in for a moment, then went on: "We'd like to talk to you about him, then take a look through his room, maybe find out a little more about him, maybe something to help us find out who did it."

"Oh my, oh my," Carter said, halfway talking to himself, "That comes as a surprise. Who do you suppose would do a thing like that?"

Lew brought Carter back from wherever his thoughts were leading him. "That's what we're here for, Mr. Carter, we'd like to know whatever you can tell us. For openers, how long has he lived here, and, uh, do you know where he came from?"

Carter walked over to a wooden pigeonhole desk and took down a grey and red ledger. "It should be here, I got this book when we first moved here in 1958, and I've always kept track of ... Here it is, he paid his first rent in July 1992, for apartment 303. Paid up every month, right on time. Don't know as I could tell you where he worked and all, only that he was quiet, paid his rent on time, didn't never make any trouble. Didn't have no friends over either, that I ever recall, but then seems like he didn't make friends easy anyway. Might have spent some time with 104, that's Ernie Houston, he's in a wheelchair, but nobody else I can recall. Like I said, he never gave no trouble or anything, and he was always real quiet. Come to think of it, most times you'd never even know he was around. Never did pay much attention to him. I'm sorry he's dead and all, and I guess I ought to say we'll miss him, but there really isn't even very much to miss." Carter's eyes went out of focus as he turned his thoughts inward. "Still, nobody ought to get killed like that. Terrible thing. Wonder who'd do such a thing like that? The world sure gets worse every day. Used to be safe around here, being midtown and all, but there's no guarantee any more. I'd move, but this is all there is. And when I'm gone, our kids, they don't even live in the city any more, they'll probably just sell this place off ..."

"If we can continue, Mr. Carter, would you show us his apartment? We'd like to get as much information as we can," Lew said.

Carter paused, "Are you sure it's all right? I mean, do you need court papers or anything? I always thought you needed a search warrant, or something, to do that."

Dan's bland gaze slid over Carter's head, refusing to meet Lew's eyes. The pressure of teeth clamped on the inside of his upper lip was evident. "Yessir, ordinarily you do, and if it'd make you feel better about it we can go get one, but since he's a victim," Lew paused to let that thought sink in, then continued, "instead of a suspect, it's not like we'd need a lot of legalities. In fact, having you there as a witness that we aren't going to steal anything, that'd make us feel better about it."

A more worried look creased Carter's face. "Oh my, why would policemen want to steal anything? That's silly; who'd do a thing like that?"

This time Dan's eyes rolled skyward as Lew continued, "Well, we'd feel a lot better if you'd assist us. Will you do that, sir?"

Carter's voice firmed, and he looked Lew straight in the eye.

"Of course I'll help. Let's go upstairs, and I'll open up for you." As he started to move, Carter pulled a key ring out of his pocket, extending the spring-loaded chain. "I always keep the keys right here. Let's go."

They climbed the central stairs in the hallway, Lew noting the worn wood that showed the effects of over a half-century of use. Dan observed the absence of graffiti that suggested some level of care by the occupants, and the cooking smells that always seemed to embed themselves in the woodwork of apartment buildings. At the top they turned to the rear, stopping at 303.

Carter opened the door, holding it for the two detectives. "This's it," he said unnecessarily.

With the habits ingrained from years of practice, they split up to search the apartment. Lew turned to his right in the living room and examined the wooden bookcase next to the doorway. Dan walked through to the bedroom.

"When you're doing a search," the voice of an academy lecturer came back to Lew's mind, "you need a reliable pattern to lend consistency and thoroughness." Lew had once missed a gun that almost cost him his life, when a woman tried to shoot him after apparently surrendering. He'd also lost a couple of cases in the beginning when he missed evidence that could have wrapped up a case. Since then, he'd learned a system that he used every time. No matter if it was a crime scene search of an apartment for evidence, or even a quick shakedown of a room in which a suspect was apprehended, he stuck to his routine. And whenever he had the opportunity to play visiting professor at the academy, he touted the virtues of his particular system. Counterclockwise sweeps, starting at your immediate right at the door and moving left. The high line covers the ceiling and walls down to eye level; the middle line covers from eye level down to knee level, and the low line covers from knee level down, as well as the floor. Lew worked the pattern, top, middle, bottom, right to left, top, middle, bottom, right to left, missing nothing.

As he went through the room he noted the signs of habitation; no indications of more than one occupant, no signs of a woman, the clothing, magazines and newspapers here and there telling him something of the character of the occupant. Mail on a credenza consisting mostly of marketing pitches, most directed to "Occupant."

By the time he was halfway through the room, Lew knew what Albert's taste in outerwear was, what his reading preferences were (crime and espionage adventure stories, several "Soldier of Fortune" magazines), the fact that he had a complete set of "The Destroyer" series, and that he was behind in his payments to a local finance company.

Dan had better luck in the bedroom. Starting with the same basic system, he worked through the dresser at the right of the bedroom door. Handkerchiefs, junk jewelry and ankle-length socks, plaids, solids and whites. Jockey shorts and vee-neck undershirts. Plaid polycotton short-sleeved sport shirts. Forty-four rounds of .44 magnum ammunition. An Outer's gun cleaning kit, suitable for .44 and .45 caliber, according to the lid. A literary masterpiece entitled, "Nazi Sluts in Heat" and another all-time favorite, "Acapulco Party Girls," both with dog-eared pages. Dan rifled through the pages, unimpressed with the gynecological photography, then went through the remaining drawers. He found more clothing, more old socks, worn out and mismatched; all the accumulation of things that find their way into dresser drawers and that the owner knows he will neither use nor throw away. As he turned his attention from the dresser to a small desk, the first thing to catch his eye was the scrapbook on top of a small pile of newspapers. The first page contained a hand-printed poem:

> "All you evil, quake with fear,
> When from the dark my name you hear,
> You who trample human dreams,
> Your world is not as smooth as it seems.
> Revenge and justice and I are one,
> Power flows from the barrel of my gun."

"Hold your cards, ladies," Dan murmured, "we may have a Bingo."

The remaining pages of the scrapbook contained clippings from both the morning and evening papers. They dated back about two years' worth, and as he leafed through them he recognized most of the stories. Almost all pertained to homicides, although a few were clearly accidental deaths. As Dan read further through the book, he saw clippings with phrases underlined in red, such as "no immediate leads," "unknown persons" and "lack of evidence."

"Yep," he whispered, "looks like we got a good bingo." He raised his voice: "Yo, Lew, come check this out."

"What's up?" Lew asked, as he entered the room.

"Here we go, Bro, read what our little friend's been up to."

Lew leaned over the desk reading, then, absorbed, pulled out the chair and sat down. Five minutes later he looked up at his partner. "Looks good for it, doesn't he?"

"Bigger'n shit, Bro. Here's his ammunition, his gun cleaning kit; this dude looks good, good, good. Let's finish tossing this place, grab what we need, and make it out of here."

The bedroom closet yielded a shoulder holster for a .38, but no gun. Under the bed they found a footlocker containing more old clothing, a black ninja costume and an M-1 carbine, neatly wrapped in another black cloth. "Jesus, Dan, this sonofabitch covered all the damn bases. Do you remember, were any of the shoots done with a GI carbine?"

"Yeah, I think so. But what the hell does this ninja shit have to do with it?" He looked up at Carter, who was standing there amazed. "Mr. Carter, have you ever seen any of this before? Have you ever heard him talk about any weapons, or maybe any karate classes or anything like that?"

"No, this all comes as a surprise to me. Now, who'd want to have things like this? Rifles and all, oh my. Oh my."

Lew stood, his hands full. "We'll have to take these items with us, Mr. Carter. We'll write you out a receipt for them so you won't be accused of holding his effects or anything. That all right with you?"

"Yes, I suppose so, but I don't know who'd want those sort of things anyway. I'm not sure if he had any relatives here, or anything. I'm just not sure what to do. It's all so very ..." his voice trailed off.

"We get done here, let's go have a talk with, what did you say his name was, Mr. Carter?"

"Houston, Ernie Houston. In 104," Carter answered.

The evidence tags took about 10 minutes to fill out. Each had space for a case number, a date, time, description of the evidentiary item, a location where the item was found, the name of the collecting officer and an optional signature element for the person from whom the item might be taken if it were seized from an individual. Thereafter, the rest of the tag had room for a series of signatures and dates to reflect the chain of custody and a serial-numbered portion to be given as a receipt, if necessary. When they were done, they watched Carter re-lock the door and went to their car, where they locked the items in the trunk. After they were sure the trunk was secured, they walked back in, heading for apartment 104.

Their knock was answered immediately. "In!" They walked into the living room and saw Ernie Houston. Somehow they had both expected to see an older man, retired, wheelchair-bound, whiling his days away, probably with an old cat or dog to keep him company. Instead, they found a large muscular man who could have been in his late 30s to early 40s, sitting behind a desk, wearing an olive drab T-shirt emblazoned with a grinning beret-clad skull and the motto, "Killer by Trade, Lover by Choice." He was talking on the telephone while tapping the point of a bayonet-shaped letter opener on the desk pad with the other hand.

"Look, Senator, I don't mind giving an interview to the papers on this, and I damn sure don't mind telling the media you were uncooperative ... Yeah, you got it ... Nope, not a threat at all, Senator, you can regard it as a promise ... Yeah, well, you just do that if you think you can, but how are you gonna look, taking on a disabled vet in a wheelchair, huh? Yeah, particularly since you weren't there ... Hey, I'm perfectly willing to remind the electorate that you were in divinity school until the draft was over ... Ah, struck a nerve there, did I? ... Look, I'll use the other thing, too, if I have to, and you know that'll blow your career out like a match ... What was that line from 'Gone with The Wind?' 'Frankly, my dear, I don't give a damn'" ... No, I don't really want to, but I will if I have ... Okay, they say politics is the art of the possible, so show me what's possible ... Yeah, you get the outreach centers going again ... Yeah, then maybe we can ... No way, baby, no staff, no assistants. Just you and me, eyeball to eyeball on this, no go-betweens ... Yeah ... Yeah ... Okay, that's acceptable. We'll work from there ... Okay. I'll be expecting your call ... Of course, where the hell else am I gonna go? ... Okay, Senator, we all appreciate your concern and assistance on this ... Yeah, thanks ... Okay, you have a good day, too ... Bye."

He hung up the phone and looked up. "Fuckin' hypocrite. Concerned as all hell, just as long as you don't ask him to come through for you. Well, this time he just stuck his dick in the chainsaw. You guys here about the outreach program? Agent Orange? You look pretty healthy to me. Shit, everybody looks pretty healthy to me. What can I help you guys with?" He snapped the wheelchair to where they were standing and grasped Lew's hand in a flesh-colored bear trap. "I'm Ernie Houston; you're?"

"Cops. I'm Lew Perkins, this's my partner, Dan Perkins. We're not related, thank you, and we're here to ask you about Albert Yaschew, okay?" Lew took a short breath and plunged on, trying to retain what he knew would be tenuous control of the conversation. "Albert Yaschew was shot and killed last night, and we need to learn as much as we can about him. From what we've gathered so far, we understand he used to visit with you some."

"Oh. Okay, for a minute there I thought you guys were vets. We're getting our act together, sort of doing for ourselves what nobody'd help us do before. You both look to be the right age," he said, looking closely at their faces. Were you there?"

Dan answered first. "Hundred and First, '67 to '68, all over hell and Two Corps. Which sometimes was the same thing."

"Mine was a little more complicated," Lew said. "I was a spook, worked the Central Lowlands, didn't have any particular home. Maybe Phan Rang."

"Yeah, I knew your guys, we'd use your information every so often. You guys there for Tet?"

The answer from them both was swift in coming.

"Waxed their ass, didn't we?"

"Yeah," Houston confirmed, "I used to wonder what the hell war the damn press was covering. Sure as shit wasn't the same one we were fighting. Ah, well, fuck it. That was a long time ago. So what can I do for you? You say Al Yaschew's dead?"

"Yeah," Dan said, "he was killed last night, in front of the Midtowner Lounge. We need to learn as much as we can about him, maybe get some line on the how, the who, you know, whatever we can find out ..."

"Well, shit, that's a hard break. How'd the little guy get it?" Houston leaned back in his chair, pensive. "I guess I'll miss him. Poor little bastard never had anything going for him. How'd he buy it?"

Lew took up the conversation again. "He was shot, near as we can figure, breaking up an armed robbery. It looked like he took one down, then the other one got him. Do you recall him ever telling you about owning a big .44 magnum? That's what was on him when he died."

"Huh? Sit down, guys, I'll get us a beer. Let's talk about this," he said, moving his wheelchair to the side of the room.

"No, thanks," Dan demurred, "We don't want to put you out, and we won't need to stay long."

Houston looked up sharply. "Sit!" he said, more command than invitation. "I don't like to look up at people, figuratively or literally, so sit down." They sat. He rolled back and handed them a pair of Busch Lites, and when they started to protest, he silenced them with a wave. "It's the price of admission. You want information, you kill a beer with me." He grinned. "It's a tough and dirty job."

"But somebody's gotta do it; yeah, I know," Lew finished the thought.

Houston said, crisply, "Now back to business. What can I help you guys with?"

Lew carried the thread of the inquiry forward: "Whenever he'd come down here to visit, how often would that be and what would you talk about?"

Houston took a deep swallow, wiped his mouth and kneaded the can in one hand, crinkling the aluminum, as if pausing to arrange his thinking. "First off, I gotta say, yeah, I'm sorry the kid's dead. But, I also gotta say, it's shit hot, that he went out that way. I mean, all I ever saw there was another pencil-neck wimp, you know? And now, you tell me he blew away some cat before he got greased; it puts him in a whole 'nother perspective, you know? See, he used to come down here all wide-eyed, asking all sorts of wild-ass questions about 'Nam, and how Basic was, and what Jump School was like, you know, all that typical kind of shit. Whenever there'd be a couple of us around here, we'd blow smoke up his ass about all the wild things we'd done here and there. Hell, we'd make up more shit than a hundred John Wayne movies, and he'd just eat it up. You'd listen to us, each of us had to do a dozen hitches to account for just the time spent on all that grab-ass we'd talk about." His face fell. "Y'know, I wonder if, maybe if we hadn't filled him so full of bullshit, maybe he wouldn't have tried to go out there and play hero. Maybe he'd still be alive. That sucks. That really sucks."

Dan pressed: "What we're looking for right now, though, is what was he like? Did he have any real strong feelings about things? Any subjects he had a short fuse on? That sort of thing."

Houston stared up at the ceiling for a moment, then continued, "Yeah, every once in a while he'd get all hot and bothered about stuff, like injustice. Nothing very specific. It'd mainly be like people pushing other people around, people messing over people, sometimes it'd be something that happened to him personally. Like, I remember one time, he was all pissed off that he missed a promotion at wherever the hell it was that he worked at. What gave him the red-ass was that the other guy selected was bigger. Not smarter, not better, just bigger. He was pretty sensitive about that, almost took it personally, like God didn't like him or something. Now that you make me think of it, he did talk some about getting even, getting revenge, sort of the 'I'll show them' thing, you know?"

Dan and Lew could feel the tide turning for them. "Did he ever mention any plans to do something about it? Anything specific? Did he ever mention anything like going to karate classes or buying weapons, say? Did he ever mention that .44 to you?"

"Sorry, gents, you just left me behind. Far as I know, he didn't have any guns; if he did, he'd have probably come running down here for Show and Tell time, you know? Unless there's a side of him nobody saw. And that could be, sure as hell, 'cause this whole thing comes as a surprise. I'd never figure him to be the type'd actually DO anything, you know? I'd always figured he was on the sidelines of life, but never a player. That's why I'm maybe halfway pleased he went out like he did. Probably the first time he ever did something like a man."

There wasn't much else to be gotten. Albert Yaschew might have some Walter Mitty side to him, but his neighbor and his landlord didn't have an inkling. They talked for a while, finished their beers and rose to leave.

As they were closing the door, Houston called out. "Hey ... you never did ask."

66

"Thought it best not to," Dan said.

"It's okay, Perkins, it doesn't bother me any more. Day 364, a 122 millimeter rocket into the transient barracks, at Cam Ranh Bay."

As they walked up the hallway to the front door, Lew said softly, "Now that sucks. That really sucks."

Dan's answer was equally soft. "Yo, Bro."

Chapter 8

CAPTAIN Danilovitch was not immediately available, as the fussily attired new administrative assistant told them. He was in conference. After several pointed and increasingly loud and hostile questions, he deigned to tell these low-life street cops that Senior Management (they could only wonder who the hell that might be) was conferring, and that they therefore could not possibly be bothered with such peasants as they. But he would allow them a few moments of the Captain's time whenever the conference was over, and they should sit over there. Unspoken was the inference that they should wipe their clothing before being seated.

"You remember where Danilovitch comes from, Dan?"

"Yeah, some coal-mining town in Pennsylvania. Came up through the ranks. Street cop from Day One."

"Yup; what'll you bet me he shoots this fag or throws him out the window before the month's up?"

"No bet, Bro, but if he looks at me like that one more time, my ass is gonna belong to Internal Affairs, and there won't be anything left for Danilovitch to throw out the fuckin' window."

The administrative assistant sat fussing over papers and looking important for what seemed like half an hour, when the meeting finally broke up and three very worried-looking ranking cops walked out. The Chief and Commissioner paused in front of Dan and Lew, engaged them in low and earnest conversation for a moment, then continued out.

At the door, the Commissioner turned and said, "Oh, yeah, happy birthday, Dan. I'll tell Marie I saw you. She asks about you a lot." Under the stunned gaze of the administrative assistant, who was considering a change of attitude, they walked in and closed the door. Very firmly.

"How goes it, Captain, or should we ask?"

"Don't!" Danilovitch eased himself into the chair and leaned back until he could stare up at the ceiling, where he had a red thumbtack embedded. "All that keeps me sane these days is staring at that Goddamn red thumbtack and 10 deep breaths. You don't even want to know what's going on all over City Hall, much less the Commissioner's office, not to even mention this loony bin." He closed his eyes for a moment, then snapped back to an upright position with both forearms on the desktop. "All right, let's get it on. You two didn't just drop in to pass howdys with me. What've you got?"

Dan grinned. "We got maybe a line on your vigilante. You remember that Yaschew character got iced last night? Guy with the Dirty Harry gun? Or have you read the blotter yet?"

"Yeah, I read it, and it looked pretty damn thin, if you ask me. But since you didn't, go on."

"Well, we tossed his apartment just before. And this guy looks pretty good. He looks better'n anybody's got a right to look. We got a GI carbine from his apartment. Since a couple of the early shoots were done with a carbine, it's down in the lab for ballistics. We also got a bunch of .44 ammunition, mags yet, and some other martial arts shit., and a shoulder holster to a .38, which we didn't find on the premises. Soon as we find out if this dude's got a car someplace, we'll toss it. Maybe get lucky. Incidentally, the lab says they're all backed up and we got to wait our turn. You think you could get them to give us a little priority handling?"

"Consider it done. What else've you got for me?"

"We got this. Show him." Lew slowly pulled the scrapbook from under his arm and handed it to Danilovitch. "Check the poem in the front of this scrapbook. You think the shrinks'd have fun with this Yaschew?"

"Lousy fuckin' poetry," mumbled the Captain "You'd think the silly bastard would've understood meter and rhyme. What the hell, we don't need another Shakespeare, we need us a killer." As he flipped through the pages his expression became increasingly concentrated. "I'm positive these aren't all his kills. He may be responsible for some, but there're several here couldn't possibly be his.

See here? This one was cleared." He turned the page. "Whoa, check this one. He turned the book so they could see better. "Markowitz made the collar on this guy, what, a year ago. We shipped him out to New York State on an extradition when they made him good for a mob rub-out. If my memory serves, he's singing like a damn canary up there, trading everybody he knows for a deal."

"He can't be good for all these, but you're right. It does make him look good. Just on the off-chance, keep working on this angle. See what else you can dig up; maybe he runs with a group. That might explain the different weapons, if he's our boy. Maybe he's connected with the mob, after all, maybe … well, think up all the possible angles and work them over, just in case. But my basic feeling about what you've got leans the other way. I don't think we've heard the last from our vigilante. I think this question isn't closed."

As they rose to leave, Danilovitch handed Lew the scrapbook. "Oh, yeah, one more thing," he grumbled. "Dismember that pansy out there, stuff him into a file cabinet somewhere where he won't ever be found. Then tell the Civil Service Board he ran off, and find me a replacement."

They smiled. "Sorry, Captain, you gotta kill him yourself. Too much paperwork involved."

But just as they were passing the subject of their conversation's desk, Dan stage-whispered, "Well, suppose we chop him into little pieces? You think anybody'd mind?" The door closed on Lew's "Nah, too messy. How about we come back later and put him in a cement overcoat?"

The routine took two days, and came up with the following answers:

No, Albert's gun didn't do any of the others.

No, Albert's carbine didn't do anybody at all.

No, Albert didn't have a sheet.

No, Albert didn't come from here; he came from Des Moines.

Yes, Albert did have relatives.

Yes, Des Moines P.D. had notified next-of-kin.

So the question, to borrow Captain Danilovitch's phrase, stayed open. The open question was further opened for them when, at 4:49 P.M., one Macario, Tonio J., was found lying between half of a 1973 Pinto and about half of a 1968 Datsun with a very small bullet hole in his skull, five fairly good-sized envelopes of an "unidentified white powdery substance" tucked inside his shirt, and a Pinto carburetor in his hand.

Chapter 9

"OKAY, where to?" Dan asked. "You got any preferences, speak now or forever hold your peace." Lew shook his head. "Surprise me."

"How about Cobo's?"

"Yeah. We haven't been there in God knows how long, and I think I'm hungry enough to even eat his cooking."

It was only two blocks to Cobo's, an easy walk. But there had just been a departmental directive circulated, which for the third time this year prohibited the use of city vehicles for unofficial purposes. So they drove. Lew started the car, waited patiently while Dan slammed the right side door three times before it caught, and backed out of the parking slot. They parked in a loading zone, flipped down the sun visor with its printed card identifying this as a police vehicle and as such not worth the effort of ticketing since it wouldn't be paid anyway, and walked the remaining half block. As they walked, Lew identified three other unmarked units at the curb.

Cobo's was a small bar and grill run by a retired cop aided by two antique former hookers whose profession had left them some 25 years ago, and whose only remaining talents had to do with the restaurant business. Rumor had it that Cobo had gotten to know them by busting and/or sleeping with them both, over the years, on a regular basis. At this point in their lives, it made no difference, and nobody really cared enough to bring it up anyway.

As they entered the long room they passed the cash register where one of the ex-hookers was stationed.

"Hiya, Flo, how's tricks?"

"My name still ain't Flo, you asshole, and you'll never know how tricks is. Don't ask for the fish. Get the pastrami, or maybe the lasagna, it came out good today."

They walked down the room, past the long bar where Cobo presided, surrounded by police memorabilia. A rotating beacon flashed reds, whites and blues overhead, the light subdued by several years' worth of dust.

"Yo, Perkins an' Perkins, how goes it with the intellectuals these days?"

"Just the usual, Harve, fighting for truth, justice and the American Way. You?"

"Doin' okay. Weather stays off my arthritis, business stays decent, I maybe this year keep outa bankruptcy. If it wasn't for the pension … ah, what the hell, any day you wake up's a good one, right?"

"Bitch, bitch, bitch," Lew retorted, "You got the very first nickel you ever grafted, doctors'd starve to death waiting for you to bring 'em some business, you got these two hot sex machines climbin' all over your body, what the hell more do you want?"

Cobo struck a pose, held a declamatory forefinger up in the air and intoned, "Man shall not live on beer, food and pussy. There's got to be more."

"Yeah, well, you find out what else there is, gimme a call," Lew answered. "Meanwhile, that table back there reserved?" At Cobo's shrug they passed to the back of the room.

They sat at the last table, under pictures of mustachioed cops in tall hats and long, brass-buttoned tunics. Josie, the other ex-lady-of-the-evening, arrived carrying menus, water glasses and silverware individually wrapped in those oversized cloth napkins which were a part of the mystique of Cobo's. It was the only place in town where you could eat whatever you wanted without worrying about getting half of it on your clothes. She stood there expectantly, ready to go through the time-honored ritual:

"What've you got that's good, Josie?"

"Me."

"What else?"

"Her."

"What's to eat?"

"Me."

"What else?"

"Her."

74

"You serve food in this joint?"

"Only as a sideline."

"What've you got we can afford?"

"Now you're back to talkin' about food."

The ritual over, they then settled down to order. Lew asked, "Is the lasagna as good as Flo said comin' in?"

"Better. And her name still ain't Flo. What'll you have to drink?"

"Ah, just coffee, black, no sugar." Dan closed his menu, slapping it on the polished formica. "Why the hell do I read that for anyway? One of them huge beef barbeques, Josie, with lots of that Mexican sauce, and a large iced tea."

As Josie walked away, they resumed the thread of their constant subject of conversation. "The lab report came back on the auto parts guy; they got the bullet out of his skull, .22 caliber, copperjacketed, hollow point. Goes in longs, long rifles, magnums. Too smashed for a good ID, so no break there either, except he's obviously one of ours. Bad guy, dead, no leads."

"I sure as hell wish you'd get your act straight and figure out who's taking all these bad-asses down, Dan," Lew murmured, "you're screwing up my reputation as a smart cop. How the hell 'm I gonna steal the credit for this case if you don't come up with some good answers?"

"Sheeit, man, I was waitin' on you to come up with the breaker on this one. I'm too lazy and stupid for this. You either got to carry me, or we'll both get fired. We screw up, it's gonna be all your fault, Bro, 'cause I done warned you. I told you years ago that I wasn't none too bright, so don't let it come as no surprise to you now."

They grinned at each other and attacked the arriving food with both hands. As they ate, Dan idly ran his eyes over the members of the crowd he didn't know, separating the cops from the civilians. It amused him to recall that, early in his career, he'd been present when two men who'd just held up a liquor store walked in here trying to hide out somewhere for a while. It didn't help their day one bit that as they were sitting down amid a house full of cops, Cobo's police monitor behind the bar blared out their complete descriptions. Out of pity for born losers, Cobo had spotted them to their last beer of freedom. They had drunk those beers glaring at each other and surrounded by gun barrels.

* * * * * * * * *

Lew's glazed donut showed three significant bites out of it when he returned to his desk. It rested on a Police Department buck slip that read, "Good donut. See me. D.G." Lew walked down the hall, finishing what was left of his donut.

"Fees for consultations, ma boy," Grimes said, imitating W.C. Fields. "Aaaahh, yeeyass, simple fees for complex cases, aahh."

"You got something for me, Lieutenant, or are you just fakin' it to rip me off from my donuts, one by one?"

Grimes leaned back, winced, leaned to his right, and began: "You were absolutely right, Lew, there wasn't anything in those files, and if you'll walk with me through some convoluted logic, what was there was what WASN'T there. Try this on for size. All those bad guys, every one of them, wasn't convicted his last time in court. Except for one of the three gang kids in the park, each of the others recently beat the rap. They each walked on a major felony case, and each got offed later.

"I think that's what the common denominator was. And, since I've got your curiosity up now, I'll feed you one more theory, after you close my door." His voice dropped to a low rumble. As Lew returned to Grimes' desk, he turned deadly serious, his normally mobile face bereft of expression. "I'd sure be tempted to figure this killer for possibly one of our own. Maybe a cop, maybe somebody from the prosecutor's staff, maybe somebody in the judicial, like that.

"Look, these guys're getting offed after they've walked on something big. Forget the street punks for a minute, and what you've got is people who somehow got away from what they had coming to them. And there's really only two groups who'd want these scum real bad, who'd have the motive and who'd have the means of finding them afterward. After that, the rest would be fairly easy. Anybody with enough smarts can plan the how and when on a hit."

"That's some pretty bad shit, Davey," Lew said pensively. "I don't like to think we've got a bad cop. Or, Jesus, worse, a prosecuting attorney, or somebody, taking it out to the street ..."

"I don't like it either, my man, but I don't get to make the rules in this world. Who knows, maybe I'm wrong; it's just a theory anyway. Problem is, it's the best theory I've come up with, and it seems to fit pretty damn good. Couple of things I'd do, I'd start to go back over the physical evidence, see what it can tell me about this killer." He smacked a hand down on one of the file folders. "This one, the knifing here, suggests somebody left-handed, probably five-six to five-ten, some kind of a long blade, pretty thick, about an inch and three-quarters wide. Like an army bayonet, or something. And you're probably looking for someone with a pretty fair knowledge of anatomy. One thrust right into the heart, this's not your average schnook. Something else I'd do, maybe get close with the property people. It's not beyond the realm of possibility that, say, a cop would use guns already in the property room, figuring nobody'd ever look for a weapon inside the house." He tapped a pencil on his blotter. "I'd like to be wrong on this one, but for starters I'd look pretty close to home."

Lew pursed his lips. It had been a thought running around the back of his mind, but he'd so far suppressed it. Now that it was out in the open, he had to think along those lines. "Thanks, Loot, I appreciate your help. If I ever get the opportunity to return the favor and mess over your mind, just let me know."

Grimes chuckled. "You just don't appreciate that I narrowed the list of possibles down some for you. Of course, I could be wrong, in which case all you've got to sift through is the entire population of two counties. But you do what you think's right."

"Yeah, right. Well, thanks anyway. See you."

Back in the squadroom, Lew briefed Dan on what Grimes had told him. "Hey, Bro, we could have gone without that suggestion," Dan said, "but maybe he's right. It would answer some tough questions. You know anybody in the Property Room, let's take us a walk downstairs."

* * * * * * * * *

After closing the door behind him, Lew dropped his keys back into his pocket and walked into the kitchen where Mrs. Halloran from next door was bustling around the stove. In a mock-angry voice he said, "What're you doing here again Mrs. Halloran? Didn't I tell you I don't need somebody cooking and cleaning? I don't need a housekeeper. Besides, I'm not hungry."

As she handed him a beer from the refrigerator, she looked his suit over for wrinkles and stains, then said, "You don't need a house-keeper, Boyo, you need a keeper, period. I've seen what you eat. Junk. You'd die in a week without some sort of decent food as an antidote to what you swill up out there."

She picked up her own half-finished beer from next to the stove and said, "Man shall not live by beer alone, Boyo, that was what Himself used to say, and it served him for better than 70 years. And did he die of malnutrition? He did not. He died happily in his sleep, he did."

"Yeah, of cholesterol," Lew said, pulling off his coat and seating himself at the table "What's this? Pot roast again? I had that last week."

"And you'll have it again this week. Shut up and eat." She ladled a heavy portion onto his plate, moved the salad dressing closer to his place setting, then turned back toward the sink.

"You had two phone calls this afternoon, one from your ex, call-ing about the alimony. I told her you'd been kidnapped by Martians and weren't expected to return to Earth. The other was from some nice young woman; she said life is good, and she'd call you back later. Her, I told her you'd be home just about now. And if that's who I think it might be, Boyo, her earring's on your dresser top. I found it when I made up your bed. Next time, tell her to take them off, too."

Lew choked, blushed and had a minor fit. When he could look up, he saw Mrs. Halloran smiling down on him. "Be comfortable, Boyo, you're only a young buck, and you're a rascal of a cop, not a priest. You're allowed. Besides, whatever her name is, I approve. I heard the Irish in her voice." Her eyes looked off into the distance as her voice softened. "I could tell you tales, of when Himself was young ..." She snapped back to the here and now. "But I won't."

Lew waved his fork in midair. "Tell me, Mrs. Halloran, why is it you do all this for me? I mean, you cook meals, you clean up for me, make me take out my laundry, you do these things for me that, and, now, let me not get misunderstood here, but these are things of daily living, I'd do them for myself, but you do them for me. Hell, it can't be for the free beers in the icebox. Why do you do for me?"

She sat down at the table and wrapped both hands around her beer can, silent for a moment. "My parents came to this country, Lewis, during some bad times. They settled in New Jersey, in an Irish neighborhood. We lived in neighborhoods then, and you were expected to stay there, marry some nice neighborhood lad, raise your children, have them marry some neighborhood children, and so on and so forth. It was a sense of community. You didn't wander too far away, even if you had friends or relatives in other neighborhoods and other cities. It was a terrible big thing, me comin' here with Himself, an' leavin' the neighborhood. That was a topic of conversation for almost a year, it was. Maybe it's hard for your generation to understand, being mobile and all, but we had roots in our neighborhoods. You haven't any roots. You've family in a place you call 'back home,' and you go from city to city, following a job or a promotion and moving on that way to the next place and the next place, without a look back. Understand me, Lewis, I'm not condemning your way, I'm just after comparing it with mine."

"And in those neighborhoods, you see, parents used to always look out for us, and for other parents' children as well. It was a sense of community. It made for a terrible big family, but you might say that parents were interchangeable. Not like it is today, where each parent cares only about his own. If you were from the neighborhood and you were doing something wrong, POW!" She swung her hand, "Any parent would likely rap you one. And you didn't complain to your own parents, 'cause, first, you knew you'd done wrong. Second, you were likely to get it again from them when they found out what it was you were doing that you got it for the first time."

"Now, that's not to say every adult went around hittin' every kid either. Right was right and wrong was wrong, and some parent who found out his kid got hit undeservingly, he'd just go down the street, call out whoever'd done it, and there'd be hell to pay, that's for sure. Puttin' discipline onto a child was serious business, and you always made sure you were right. We all knew each other and we all knew what was right and what was wrong. That's how it was for discipline, and that's how it was for helpin' or doin' for others."

"If your mother was sick, or havin' a baby, you didn't miss a meal. If your father was out of work, there'd be a shirt comin' to you from somewhere. When all the neighborhood children were goin' to the Saturday picture show, there'd be a dime for you somewhere, so you'd not be the only one not to go. There'd be orphan children never missed a hug or a spankin' for lack of a parent."

"It wasn't special, it was just that we had a sense of community, and that was the way of it. Maybe it doesn't fit the same way anymore, what with them hippies and yuppies, they either don't want to be part of life or they want to own it all. Sometimes I feel real sorry for them, Lewis, because all they'll ever really have in this world is each other, and they're afraid to give to each other. They don't understand loyalty, they don't understand commitment to anything but themselves. They work from something that maybe our generation gave to them, but someplace along the way it got misunderstood. They think it's all for them, but it's all take and no give. They have great expectations, Lewis, in one direction only. Anyway, you wanted to know why I do for you. That's part of the why. In our generation, it's a thing that you do, because it's the right thing, not because you get anything out of it."

"You still don't understand it well, do you? Then let me put it this way. I mother because I'm a mother, for the same reasons you're a cop. We are what we do, me boyo, and that's that." She drained her beer and placed it on the table with a thump. "Now eat your dinner, it's gettin' cold. And that nice young colleen'll be callin' you any minute now."

* * * * * * * * *

Lew was rarely late to work. Dan could usually walk in and find him already seated there, his tie and jacket a random combination of colors, spilling half a jelly donut down his shirt front, a paper cup of coffee in one hand which would usually be also holding a file. So it was with surprise, expressed verbally as well as with lifted eyebrows, that Dan watched Lew saunter through the squadroom. His sport jacket surrounded a color-coordinated tie, and when he took it off at his desk, Dan almost laughed out loud when he noticed the shirt. White broadcloth, button-down collar, and with his initials delicately monogrammed over the pocket.

"Whooee, boy, you done got yo'self connected with some high-tone woman, she gettin' yo' white ass civilized," he said. Lew looked at Dan, all wide-eyed and innocent. "Who, me? What? Something different around here? What's going on, Dan?"

"Don't who me, home boy, you never owned a tie like that in your life, much less a classy-looking shirt, with a monogram yet. That says woman."

Lew grinned back at Dan. "Yeah, why not? You remember that jumper, I forgot to get her name? Well, I ran into her in a bar a little while back, and we got to know each other a little. Maybe it's unprofessional, but on a personal basis, I like her. She likes me. The shirt and tie are a gift, no particular reason, she just thought I'd like it. What do you think?"

Dan winked. "I think maybe you got lucky, partner. I think maybe it's time you got somebody back in your life. If she's what's happening, go to it. And see if she'll help you pick out some suits. I need you to look good, my man; otherwise you detract from my image."

"That's what I like about you, partner," Lew flashed, as he sat down, "you're always so concerned about me."

"Just all heart, babe, just all heart. Hey, my man," he said, "just remember, though. We're cops. You're a cop, she's a civilian. That don't always spell good things for everybody. Be careful, Bro, don't get hurt, huh?"

Lew's answer was measured and thoughtful. "I hear what you're saying. I think maybe we're good for each other, Dan. Anyway, for as long as it lasts, this's a good thing. It's not like we're kids; in fact, she's five years older than I am. I don't know how to explain it to you, but it's like, it's a comfortable thing. At this point, we're sort of healing each other, and from there, who knows?"

"Okay, Bro, I trust your judgment, only just don't get hurt. What say," Dan added, in a change of pace, "let's go play cops for a while?"

By this time Lew had eaten half his donut, leaning exaggeratedly forward and holding a napkin in his other hand to protect his new shirt. "Yeah, why not? Hey, here's what I figure we can do with the bad cop possibilities ..."

Chapter 10

LEW walked back to their desks holding a 50-page computer print-out. "Here it is. Every citizen complaint and departmental violation report about a cop for the last five years. Everything from alleged impolite to murder one."

Dan looked closely at the stack and whistled. "I didn't figure on this many. Man, this says something."

"Not necessarily. While it was running, I scanned it for a while. Most of these are minor complaints, petty shit, unfounded, non-specific, stuff like that. We sort those out of this list and we'll probably get ten percent that're legitimate beefs. Then, we'll be looking at maybe ten percent of those that'll fit what we're looking for. So really all we've got here is one percent probability of bad cops. And hell, that's less than the standard distribution on a bell-shaped curve. You know how that goes."

Dan waved a handful of files. "Can you handle it? I'm still running through these for names on the scenes, call-ins, backups and first-to-arrive."

"Yeah, sure," Lew answered, "no problems here. Besides, it'll satisfy my nosiness and curiosity to find out what our less angelic brethren have been up to. Who knows? I may even run across your name in here." Lew looked at Dan with all the sincerity of a Congressman. "Save me the trouble, Dan, just confess now. If you're innocent you have nothing to fear, otherwise we'll just have to convict you anyway."

"Okay, Bro, I confess. Book me for reckless fornication."

"Bullshit. You couldn't get laid if you used hundred-dollar bills as a calling card."

"Oh, yeah? Listen, Bro, I'd have to leave town to get a strange piece."

Dan dropped his head to the files, mumbling just loud enough for Lew to hear. "Man, let them white boys get a little leg, they think they've discovered the only one there is."

Lew slammed his hand down on the desk. "You mean there's others? Hot damn!"

At the end of 30 minutes, Lew slid a handwritten list of names across to Dan. "Okay, here's the names on the solid complaints; the tally-marks indicate the number of times a man's name came up in the list. We got a few guys here that're definitely not nice people. I wonder how the hell they stay on the force."

Dan sighed. "The world catches up with them eventually, Bro. Nobody ever gets away with it all." An hour's worth of cross-checking yielded three names who were subjects of substantive complaints and who showed up in the files as having been, for one reason or another, at the scene of at least one killing.

Lew pushed himself away from the desk. "What do you say we go visit some sources, see what's on the street, then have lunch? I need to do some shopping, too."

"You're on, Bro," Dan said, as he stood up and reached for his coat. "We hit the street, we scarf up some, say, how about some Mexican, then we'll do your shopping. I need to swing by the dry cleaner's, too. You ought to try that sometime. Keeps the flies from gathering on your lapels."

* * * * * * * * *

Just because you've been assigned a particular case, it doesn't mean you get to spend all your time on it alone. Maybe they can get away with that on television, but Dan and Lew knew better. Real police departments don't have unlimited resources, which means that you do a lot of things you'd rather not. Like catching your share of squeals. Like arson, rape, murder, armed robbery, bicycle theft and lots and lots of burglaries.

So it went, the long summer days having shortened into autumn, temperatures going down, and as it got colder, the nature of crimes changed from crimes against persons to crimes against property. Or at least that's how it seemed. By Labor Day, there seemed to be fewer people sitting on the curb in front of a bar on Fridays, picking beer bottle out of their eyebrows. There seemed to be fewer people with multiple stab wounds showing up at the emergency room of County General, who weren't anyplace, weren't doing anything and just suddenly noticed that they were bleeding from those multiple stab wounds, inflicted who-knows-how.

But there did seem to be a whole rash of burglaries, particularly at the fringe of the commercial area, between Broad and Main.

Which is why Lew and Dan were spending an absolutely delightful evening, drinking cold coffee and eating stale sandwiches and looking out a second-floor loft window down the alley at four loading dock doors. One of Dan's informants had told him that the street noise was that Hursie Pharmaceuticals was going to become an inadvertent supplier to a couple of independent entrepreneurs. This same informant had once also told Dan that the armed robber specializing in oriental restaurants was about to order money to go from a particular Chinese restaurant. If you really like egg rolls, as Dan did, you can consume an awful lot of them during a stakeout. And if you catch your man, as they had that night, the proprietor would like to offer you your weight in egg rolls. As he had that night.

So, when you get good information, you generally treat it well, and you take it seriously. Which is why, for the third night running, they were wishing this were another restaurant heist. The food's better. Lew watched with a flicker of interest as two shapes moved down the alley. He dismissed them when they made it to the other end without so much as engaging in a misdemeanor Okay, so he thought, maybe this's the slack season. Besides, as they walked under a street light he could see that they were elderly. Nope, no burglars there; they looked like the type wouldn't even spit on the sidewalk. But over there now, the pickup truck that just doused its lights and was crawling down the alley, that looked more like customers. Them there kind of guys, well, they just naturally had to be clients. "Get ready, Dan, this looks like it," he whispered.

"What're you whispering for? We're inside on the second floor, they're outside, and downstairs at that."

"Stop the Goddamn nitpicking and come look." Dan eased over to the window, still holding the Styrofoam cup with its cargo of semi-cold paint remover.

"Where?"

"Third building, pickup truck just stopped. Came in with his lights out."

Night vision is a tricky thing. It takes a while for your eyes to develop it each time, and then, because of the difference between the rods and cones, the specific cells which convert light to nerve impulses in your retina, you can't see something at night if you stare directly at it. Dan knew all of this, which is why he refocused his eyes, scanned slowly over the entire area, and then looked slightly to the side of the point he was interested in, just in time to make out two occupants getting out of the truck. As he drifted his focal point around, sweeping the area, he saw the two huddle at one of Hursie's loading doors.

"Yup, that'll be them. Are you ready?"

"Two more minutes, then we do it. Let them get inside, maybe even get the first box into the truck, we get them cold." They waited. Eventually the first box, accompanied by two now-felons, made its way to the pickup. Dan spoke softly into the small radio unit he'd checked out from the squadroom's equipment locker. Another minute of conversation and he got up, stretched and shifted his revolver to a slightly less uncomfortable position on his hip. "Okay, they're on the way. We move in slow, and we'll have backup. Should be a piece of cake."

And so it was, although the two burglars would have preferred to pass on it. They walked out the door, each with a box in his arms, and each had an instant heart attack when the hand fell on his shoulder. That wasn't bad enough, it just had to be made worse by the two sets of headlights that also went on, freezing them like frogs in a pond. The frisk, the reading of the rights, the application of "restraints," otherwise known as handcuffs, and the leisurely call-in, to relay for the responsible person for Hursie, all took less than ten minutes. Fast, easy, no strain, no pain.

Their mood was even further lightened when one of the perps started his end of the conversation with, "He made me do it!" and then proceeded to dump all over his partner, beginning with the first job they'd ever pulled. Some days, Dan thought, nothing goes right; some days, you just can't miss. He'd just slammed the door of the cruiser and was turning away from the car when he heard it. The absolutely unmistakable sound of about 20 rounds going off, in full automatic.

They hit the end of the alley at full speed, sprinting ahead of the cruisers, their shadows magnified by the headlights. And then they stopped dead. Sometimes you can't tell where a particular sound came from, and this happened to be one of those times. "Well, shit," Lew said, "where the hell did that come from?"

Slightly to their left was the five-way intersection where the diagonal of Carriage Road started, at Broad and Thirtieth. Along Carriage Road, which used to be a genteel neighborhood after the frontier days petered out in the early 1900s, the neighborhood was now undergoing what urban sociologists like to call "cultural revitalization." That meant it had been discovered by the Yuppies. They were renovating essentially structurally sound slum houses, parking their BMWs and Volvos tail-to-nose with 15-year-old Ford station wagons, junked-out Plymouths and rusty Cadillacs.

The smell of brie cheese mingled with ribs; white wine competed with Thunderbird and Ripple. Dewey Stevens, down here, was not the maker of fine Scotch. Dewey Stevens, down here, was the name of a guy maybe used to live on the next block, went to prison a couple years ago. It also meant that the people who lived here because they couldn't afford to live anyplace else were about not to be able to afford this place either. But at the moment it was "ethnically diverse," which meant that it belonged to the Yuppies and their real estate agents and interior decorators by day. At night it was another story.

Dan scanned both directions, then took off toward Carriage Road with Lew puffing along behind him, and two police cars, lights now flashing, bringing up the rear. They cut hard right to make the acute angle onto Carriage Road, leaving the sidewalk so as to better scan the area for trouble.

The fourth building in was a three-story red brick, with two storefronts (Ajax Bail Bonds, 24 hour service, Ma's Downhome BBQ) from which light spilled onto the street. As they arrived that far down, the light showed them two small boys, probably neither over nine years old, coming out of the alley just past Mom's.

"Hey, man, the dude's dead in there," one of them said. The

other, being quite a bit more cool about it, said, "Yeah, man, somebody iced him. Hey, man, don't shoot, huh?"

Lew wasn't aware until then that he'd drawn his gun, but he let it precede him into the mouth of the alley, for the first four feet. Behind him the rising babble of voices told him that the neighborhood now considered it safe to come up from under tables, behind doors and parked cars, and see what had happened.

"Jesus," Dan breathed, "will you look at that!" The flicker of the rotating red, white and blue beacons of top of the arriving patrol cars threw pulsating flashes of light over the body. Except for the fact that he was standing in the middle of a murder scene, Dan felt the lights give an air of patriotic festivity. A little late for the Fourth of July, but the sound effects and lighting were about right.

He could see that the kids were right. The dude had indeed been iced. His cream sport coat and white shirt showed what were easily half a dozen spreading blotches of blood, and on the wall above where he lay there were broad red smears where the force of the bullets had thrown him before he slid to the ground. The open coat showed an empty shoulder holster; the nickel-plated gun lay loosely in his right hand, resting across one bent leg.

Lew bent down to touch the man's throat, feeling for a pulse, also feeling foolish halfway through the motion, since people with that many holes in them are rarely in livable shape.

Dan turned to the uniforms in the nearest car, calling instructions to them, also unnecessarily, since he could see the uniform in the passenger seat spilling a lot of agitated conversation into the mike.

"Dead, right?"

"Dead, right, Dan, just as dead as they ever get."

"Well, we couldn't have gotten here more than two, three minutes late at the max, Bro, so whoever did this cat, he's in the neighborhood right now."

The keening sound started on a low note, rapidly rose up the scale and ended in a howl of anguish that Lew had once, and only once, heard before. That was when he'd watched a patrolman wade out of the water of Tate Park Lake cradling the limp body of a three-year-old. The sound had come from its mother. He spun around from the body with the hair on the back of his neck rising and cleared the mouth of the alley in two steps.

Dan was close behind as he shifted the focus of his eyes, then froze in his tracks. Dan spoke first. "Well, sheeit," he intoned, "some scum ain't got no respect for BMWs."

In the light they could see three bullet holes: two had punched in through the right side window, removing the windshield on the way out. The third had violated the chastity of the right door panel and had probably also brutally penetrated the expensive stereo rig Lew just knew had to be there.

The man in the velour jogging suit held the woman in the matching velour jogging suit as she cried, rocking her back and forth and patting her on the back "It's all right, Buff, we'll have it towed away and get it fixed," he crooned. "It's all right, it's insured."

Dan and Lew exchanged deadpan glances.

"Terrible."

"Vandals."

"Scum."

"Low-lifes, to do such a thing."

"Look at it this way, Bro," Dan said reasonably, "every cloud has its silver lining. Whoever committed such a dastardly deed on this here poor defenseless BMW just told us something. Now we know he shot from inside this alley; we ought to find a whole potload of brass laying in there."

By the time the homicide crew, coroner's boys, shift captain and all the assorted VIP's, IP's and P's had arrived to occasionally assist and occasionally hinder, the crowd behind the yellow plastic tapes had increased to five deep.

And, of course, none of them had seen anything at all, hadn't even heard any shots, just came wandering over after they saw the rest of the crowd. Nobody'd even been looking out their windows. It figured, at least that part of it. When it's summer the windows are open, and people are hanging out getting a breath of air and being entertained by the continuous show on the streets. When it's cold and the hawk is out, people turn their faces, their bodies and their thoughts inward where it's warm. In this autumn, this time of transition, the windows had already closed for the remainder of the year. Lew and Dan did the usual, trying to find someone in the crowd who might have seen something, heard something, anything, could give them some little piece of information they could follow to find out who had made the unknown so very dead. The reason they were dealing with an unknown became fairly clear to them within the first five minutes of their arrival at the scene. The two little kids they'd originally seen had vaporized, and the only contents of the dead man's inverted hip pocket had been a comb.

"You beat that?" Lew had mumbled, "those little bastards must've picked him clean before he quit bouncing. Shit."

"Don't knock 'em, Bro, they learnin' theyselves a trade; they gonna be politicians," Dan had answered.

"So, how come they didn't steal the gun, too, Dan?"

"Simple, Bro, you get elected, you don't need no gun after that."

As they worked the crowd, the crew from the Medical Examiner's office said that, yes, this here deceased is dead; yes, he'd died from multiple gunshot wounds, as a preliminary judgment only, pending autopsy, and yes, they'd be willing to now remove him if there wasn't anything more the crime scene boys needed. They were still working the crowd when the evidence technicians came out of the back portion of the alley holding numerous small bags, each containing some brass. All but two were of the same size. All but two were obviously fresh and shiny.

"We got 18 9 millimeter's here, and we got two .22's, look like old stuff. Maybe from the last shooting in this here alley, huh?" They looked with interest at the newer brass. Nine millimeters were a new actor on the scene. By now they knew who the victim was. His name had been Sylvester Reed, ex-pusher, ex-mugger, ex-holdup artist, ex-person. And that made all of this another one of theirs.

"Lew, this mother's equipped better than we are; he's up to automatic weapons. What the fuck's next, artillery? Bombers? Missiles?"

"No, man," Lew said, as he slapped Dan on the back, "relax. I been down the road, the Air Force still has all its missiles. This little bastard can only shoot. He can't nuke us. Yet."

"That's what I like about you, Bro, you make me feel so confident."

By now the crowd had considerably thinned out, leaving only a few black people of various ages, no yuppies ("Oooh, gross, let's go, Skip!) and two very old-looking white people, in long black overcoats, with mufflers and gloves to ward off the unseasonable cold.

"How about you folks, did you see anything?" Lew asked. "Where were you when it happened?"

In heavily accented English, the old man told Lew they'd been about a block away, and yes, they did hear the shots. He interrupted himself to speak to the old woman in a language Lew didn't recognize. He turned back to Lew when he was finished, and said, "She has little English, so I translate for her. I can tell you it was shots."

Dan asked, "How many shots did you hear? Any idea?"

The old man turned again, and they exchanged a few sentences. The woman seemed agitated to Lew, but he put it down to the shock of the killing. After all, how many nice old folks see homicides up close?

"We don't know how many shots, they were very fast. Like machine gun. This we have heard before, during the war, in Poland."

"You're Polish?" Lew asked.

"No, we are Americans. We used to be Polish, but we are now Americans. We have papers."

Dan grinned. "Americans, huh?"

"Yes!" the old man said, with a fierceness neither Dan or Lew expected. "We are Americans, as good as you, we live here for over 40 years. We bring up our children here, we even give one son to that war in Vietnam. We are good Americans."

Dan's voice softened, as he apologized for them both, then he explained. "Hey, I think it's great, it's just that all you hear is people who're Mexican-Americans, Italian-Americans, French-Americans; hell, they're even trying to call me an African-American. It's like you're supposed to be something else all the time, you can't just be an American. That was what I meant. No offense."

The old man translated for his wife, then in a softer voice, he answered Dan. "I understand. I will tell you something, young man. Citizenship is a loyalty to only one country, whatever that would be. When we came here, not just my wife and I, but all of us who walked out of hell after the war, we came out of concentration camps, displaced persons camps, all of them only jails and holding pens, and we saw when we arrived the Statue of Liberty in New York. We saw the lady with the torch, and we knew then that we would live free, that this was where good things would happen. In this

91

place we found a home, we raised our sons, we made our place in the world; we did here what no other country in the world would let us do. And I tell you this; we know the difference. We who come here from other places, we know the difference. Citizenship papers, they mean you have a ..." he paused for a moment, gathering his thoughts, "a responsibility, a price to pay for what you get. There is no half a loyalty to this country and half to another; you give it all here. We can remember the old country, remember and observe the old customs, but when we come here, this is our place. I have yet the telegram, I remember the words clear, from the Army, about our son. We have his medals, we have letters, we have his flag to remind us what we paid. We paid Captain Tadeusz Kolchinsky for this country. We paid, how is it you say, our dues. Yes, we are Americans."

The old man paused for a moment, visibly changing gears. He returned his gaze to Dan and said, "All we can tell you is there were shots, many of them. Rapid. From a machine gun. But there is nothing else we can tell you. If you are through with us, we must go."

"In just a moment," Dan said, "if you'll bear with me for just a moment. Where did you say you were at when you heard the shooting? Wait, let's back up just a moment. Can I have your names, sir, for my report?"

"I am David Kolchinsky," he spelled it out, "and this is my wife, Ruth."

"Do you live around here?"

"No, we were out for a walk, and we walked to this neighborhood; we didn't pay any attention to where we were going. We bought from a store some groceries, and we walked to here. Now, if you will let us, my wife is tired and we must go home."

Dan pressed, "Well, did you happen to see anyone in the street, say, running? We can use any help you can give us. You know how it is, crime like this hurts us all. The police department can't do it all alone, we need help from people. We need everybody who'll help. It's like you said, it's like paying dues. We all have to help to keep law and order."

Kolchinsky's voice held a note of impatience. "We can tell you nothing more than we have already told you. If we could, we would. Now, my wife is tired, I must get her home. We have seen enough blood and death in our time, we need no more. Please, I must get her out of here. We must go."

"All right," Dan conceded, "if you can't help with anything else, there's no real reason to keep you from going home. Where did you say you lived?"

"I didn't," Kolchinsky said, "but we are at the Forest Fen, the rest home. It is on Vista Parkway, in the 4300 block."

Dan hesitated, then made up his mind. "Look, it's a pretty long way from here, and like you said, your wife's pretty beat already. How about we spot you a ride home. It might make up, say, for the hairy evening. All right?"

"Thank you," Kolchinsky said, "that would be very helpful." He turned back to his wife and translated for her for a moment. She answered back in what seemed to be a worried tone, but he replied firmly enough that she seemed to give up whatever she was objecting to. "We would like that very much."

Dan called one of the uniforms over and explained what he wanted to do. The uniform smiled, then opened the back door of his cruiser with a flourish. Once they were safely in, he drove off.

David Kolchinsky helped his wife Ruth up the steps and through the front doors of the Forest Fen Retirement Home.

As they entered, Patrolman Tim Willis turned to his partner and said, "Can you beat that? Those old folks must be a thousand years old, and they're still tight, still lookin' out for each other. You check how he had his arm around her in the car? Even helped her carry the old shopping bag, or whatever, up the steps, held her arm, all that bit. Hell, me and the wife don't hang in there all that tight, after only five years."

Patrolman Ed Martin retorted, "That's because you're such a lousy scumbag, Tim. You don't deserve anybody takin' care of you. Your poor wife's just doin' penance for some terrible sin in some past life. You're her punishment. Now, if you was a nice, decent human being, say, like those nice old folks there, maybe you'd deserve better. That old couple, they probably raised their kids right, they make church every Sunday; wouldn't surprise me does she make Mass every morning. That's the type, wouldn't hurt a fly. They go through life with rosaries in one hand, one arm wrapped around each other, that's nice people." He sobered. "You know, seriously, that's nice. I wish something like that for me and Imogene when we get old, if I survive the job ..."

Willis turned down Thurman, absently eyeballing the street sides. He remarked, "Yeah, but I sure hope when we get old, we don't get to smelling all funky like that. You get a whiff of that old lady's perfume, or whatever, maybe it's just body odor, but it smelled more like something burned, almost like ... uh, oh, check that out, over there. See those two helpin' themselves to the wheels off that corvette? Get ready, partner, we're goin' back to work."

In their room, David withdrew the Uzi from Ruth's knitting bag. "I'll take this downstairs and clean it and put it away, you'll make some tea while I'm gone?"

"You sure I can handle something like that, Mister Spokesman? Maybe it's too difficult for somebody doesn't speak any English? What was it with that anyway?"

"Now, Ruth, I only said that so they shouldn't pay too much attention to you. What should I say, 'Please, mister policeman, don't pay any attention to my wife, all she's got in her bag is a machine gun?' Look, I know what I'm doing, it's just like the old days. You misdirect their attention, they'll never notice you. Soldiers or policemen, it's the same thing."

Ruth sighed, then waved both her hands at him in a characteristic gesture of annoyance and resignation. "Go, go, go. I'll make tea."

Chapter 11

DAN walked into the squadroom carrying a stack of files. "You wouldn't believe all the shit you have to go through to get these, Lew. I had to sign away my life. Should have just reviewed them up there, and to hell with it. Nice tie. Another present?"

"Nope. We did a little shopping, she helped me pick it out. You like? It's by some French designer, costs like crazy."

"Yeah, but it upgrades your image. That lady's doing good things for you, Bro, don't lose her."

"Have no fear of that, my man, she does good things for me inside as well as out. No plans to let her get away. What've you got here?"

"This's 14 camouflage files, guys I picked up just to fill out a list, and our three best possibles off the computer printout." Dan pulled out the relevant three and set the others aside. "What we got here is Hugo Fairfield, Walter Canby and Edward Camacho. Any one of whom, you might say, could be our vigilante. Let's dig in."

The files didn't take all that long to reveal what they held. Dan laid them out on his desktop and slapped each with his hand. "Okay, partner, here we go. This's Hugo Fairfield. His string of complaints runs for about four years, and he seems to be getting nastier. Reason? Easy. His sister was shot in a liquor store holdup, also about four years ago. She took a bullet in the brain, went into a coma and never recovered. Departmental chaplain, psychiatrist, all the usual people worked with him. Apparently didn't do any good. Here's a guy with a reason. Here's also a guy with superior means to do it, too, Bro. He was on the SWAT team for about six months, before they took him off as psychologically unsuitable. Don't ask how he got on in the first place."

"This one's Walter Canby. How the hell he ever became a cop I don't know. He's your basic sourball, got no respect for anything or anybody. Seems to believe the way you do police work is to bust heads. He's been passed over for promotion consistently, and the way his file reads, he'll never make Sergeant. He'd likely be able to do these guys, then go home and sleep like a baby. He's got it all, too. You remember the old SIU, the Special Investigative Unit? Well, Canby was on it in his younger days. When Internal Affairs busted it up, he was one of those who escaped jail or being fired, but he was as dirty as the rest. The only difference was, they couldn't pin anything substantial on him. But he smells good for this."

Lew recalled his early days on the force, when the SIU was considered the elite unit. Major cases were deferred to them. They handled all the cases involving narcotics traffic, over some minimum limit Lew couldn't remember. They were answerable to virtually no one, and they took an almost childish delight in breaking rules. They inspired fear, resentment and ambition. Every young cop aspired to the SIU. They were the best; they were society's avenging angels. But somewhere along the way, they became like those they were supposed to bring in.

According to testimony at the Grand Jury proceedings, it began with using narcotics seized from street dealers, to retain control over users who would trade information to sustain their habits. From there, they began to use bribery money to pay informants when departmental funds ran thin. Sometime thereafter, the uses of those narcotics and funds became personalized. At the end, they were shown to be no better than the subjects of their investigations. Several members of the SIU went to prison, most were fired, a few were reassigned. In looking back, Lew considered it a lucky break that he'd been too junior to volunteer for the SIU.

"Third guy — here's one I feel sorry for — Walter Camacho. About a year ago a couple of hyped-up dopers took down one of those all-night gas stations, wrecked the safe trying to get the good money, then beat the hell out of the attendant for the fun of it. They took off with a small amount of cash. The rough part is, they lost it going over the North Trafficway overpass, jumped the railing and came down right on top of his wife's car. Killed the wife and two daughters; the punks got minor injuries. They're away for nine years. Not much of a trade, three years per life. Anyway, right after this all happened, he took it out on a drunk. He got a three-day for it, and since then hasn't done anything overt. But if you want a guy with a reason, Camacho's got as good a reason as any."

"So, okay, we got three good-looking possibles. What's to work with?" Dan scribbled for a moment. "Here's their addresses, I think we need to next go through duty rosters, see who's on what shifts. I'd like to do a quick neighborhood check, see if we get anything out of that. Then let's go out and lean on every source we got. Hard. Somebody knows something. Somebody saw something. We just haven't gotten next to the right source yet. See, where all these bad guys go is where most of our snitches go. Propinquity, my man, is where it's gonna come from. Somebody gets next to somebody, somebody gets loose at the mouth. Right now, I get two good flashes. What say let's look up the records, see who's recently beat the rap for something, read his file looking for these three names, and then, if that works out, spend some night hours on whoever looks good. Your lady may not like that, Bro, but we may be stuck with it."

Lew neatly folded the computer printouts, then laid them in the bottom of his personal drawer and locked it. "Yeah, who the hell knows, maybe we get lucky yet."

* * * * * * * * *

Dan's face was a study in outrage. "Aw, c'mon, Ray, this sucks. This has to be the worst timing you've ever pulled. I'm supposed to be taking some vacation time, and you want me to hang around the damn courthouse to testify? Goddamn, man, gimme a break!" Assistant Prosecuting Attorney Ray Salerno drew himself up to his full five-six, pulled his considerable girth in a little bit, then thought better of his approach and settled into a more relaxed stance, complete with conciliatory manner. "I understand how you feel, Dan, and if I could, I'd skip your testimony and just go with Lew's, but I really need you on this one, particularly in sequence, so as to get the best effect. He was your collar, you got the evidence, and as near as he ever came to a damaging statement was in your presence. Otherwise, we got circumstantial evidence only, and some impeachable witnesses. If we're gonna get this guy off the street, we need an absolutely perfect presentation, a steamroller. This guy's gone out and hired one of those six-figure lawyers who's a combination Oliver Wendell Holmes, P.T. Barnum and Atilla the Hun all rolled into one. Hell, you know how it goes. He gets to pick and choose among who to use as jurors, what evidence to jump on, who to present as the best witnesses, the whole ball of wax. You name it, it works for his side. Me, all I got is some circumstantial, some impeachable testimony from those hairballs he was dealing with, and then try to spread two cops' testimony to do damn near the whole job. I need you guys because you're the only solid citizens with positive testimony that there is in this case. And let's face it, Dan," he cajoled, "you really want to see him go away, maybe even more than I do. Tell you what: let's agree that you'll be there for this one, and I can offer you a certain secluded cabin down at the lake, fully stocked, any time you want it, for however long of a vacation, complete with bass boat? Huh?" He waggled his eyebrows like a cartoon character. "Deal?"

"It's too cold to go fishing, Ray."

"So, who says you have to go fishing? Read my lips: Cabin. Secluded. Quiet. Yours. Now, does that paint a picture in your mind, or do I have to describe the fireplace, the bearskin rug in front of it, shall I hum a little Mantovani, maybe three bars of Johnny Mathis? Good swap, my man, all you gotta do is your civic duty ..."

"You're a conniving bastard, Ray."

"Of course. That's the first thing they taught me in law school. Now, let's run over this thing again ..."

The subject of this discussion, one Marty Ray Lane, was at that moment resting from his arduous labors of the previous night. What he was actually doing was sitting in the front seat of his customized 1985 stretched Continental, recently purchased from an airport limo company that went bust. He considered the average pimpmobile beneath his dignity, but this was all right. He sat there with the stereo turned up, watching four otherwise unemployables slop soap suds on a car in the car wash he used as a front.

The current object of his affections sat across from him as he preened himself and explained the facts of life:

"What it is, Baby, is that I've got all these contacts built up, all family. We're all related, so we watch out for each other. Nobody sells nobody else, and everybody plugged in gets his fair share. And since all the end men, the retailers, they need as well as sell, I got a lock on the product. With my kind of organization and a good supply at the right prices, always pass around the bread in the right places, I got it all. I can afford one of those three-piece-suit lawyers, carries a square briefcase and a lot of weight, to get me off. Shit, he thinks he's big stuff, I can afford to buy and sell him. Thinks he's doin' me a favor, I paid more for an airplane we dumped after one run. He's just another business expense. If I was payin' taxes, I'd be able to write him off as a deduction for professional services. Yeah, I'll be there on Thursday, baby. I never jump bail. I'll be there to go in, run through the system, and walk right back out. See, you hang in there with a winner, everything works out. Now, how's about Vegas afterward, just to celebrate?"

* * * * * * * * * *

When you're bored, just about anything to amuse will do. So after telling the prosecutor's clerk and the bailiff where he'd be, Dan strolled down the hall to Domestic Court and had himself a seat in the back. After hearing two amicables and one cross-complaint divorce, followed by three adoptions, he decided two things: the world does seem to balance out, and Domestic court just ain't as exciting as it is on TV. Still bored stiff, he walked out, checked in with the clerk ("How're we doin'?" "Pretty slow, but you're likely to be up at any moment." "Yeah, you said that an hour ago") and elevatored up to Division 10, Criminal Court.

Once out of the elevator, he turned down the short hall and pushed his way through the padded double doors. Out of habit he tiptoed, although the entire room was carpeted. He moved to the last row of bench seats, where he was the recipient of a sharp look from an elderly lady who had to move her knitting to make room for him.

Each courtroom in the building was slightly different. Over the past year a redecorating effort had taken place, and Division 10, the turf of The Honorable Frederick H. Thorley, was one of the most recent. As his eyes scanned over the room he noticed everything appeared to have been refurbished except the American flag. Its blue field had been faded out to a weak, almost lavender hue, and the thought struck him that this flag didn't belong here. The court's windows faced to the north. Sunlight couldn't possibly have faded it.

Dan's irreverent sense of humor sneak-attacked him again, as it showed him a life-size vision of The Honorable, black robes billowing in the windstream, making his getaway from another courtroom with the stolen flag fluttering from its pole over his shoulder. The involuntary snicker caught him yet another sharp look. It was pretty plain that the lady didn't appreciate someone having too good of a time in a courtroom. He stifled the mirth, then risked another of those killer looks by leaning over and asking her: "What're we watching?"

"Murder One," she whispered out of the side of her mouth. "Guy by the window knifed somebody." Her knitting needles never stopped, and for a moment she reminded him of Madame DeFarge, who used to sit knitting while she watched French aristocrats get it in the neck during the revolution there.

Dan turned his attention to the trial, mentally going fast-forward through jury selection, opening statements, ("Your Honor, members of the jury, the state is prepared to prove that this scumball killed a fine, decent, upstanding member of the community, with malice aforethought." "Your honor, members of the jury, the defense is prepared to prove that this fine, upstanding Christian gentleman didn't do any such thing. The deceased scumball tripped on his own knife and bounced 26 times"), introduction of evidence and probably crime scene technician's testimony. He tuned in to what looked like direct examination of a prosecution witness.

On an easel next to the witness stand was a detailed illustration of a street intersection, with layouts of several stores and houses. Dan could see the outline of a body sketched in, with red highlights added for effect. He absorbed the dotted lines and arrows and mentally recreated the incident, then focused on what the prosecutor was saying. "… And, Mr. Willis, where do you live?"

"At 3754 Montreal Street."

"I see. And can you tell this court, sir, where you were on the evening of July 15th, at approximately eleven o'clock?"

"Well, I was sittin' in Chumpie's Place."

"Do you know, or can you tell us, please, where Chumpie's Place is?"

"I dunno, on about 39th and Montreal, like that."

"If the court please, the specific address, for the benefit of the jury, is 3895 Montreal, if Defense Counsel will so stipulate."

Nothing happened at the Defense's table, so the assistant prosecutor continued, pointing at the chart. "This, then, is Chumpie's?"

"Uh, yeah."

"And, Mr. Willis, what were you doing there?"

"Nothin', just hangin' out."

"All right, you were hanging out at Chumpie's that night."

"Uh, yeah."

"Now, Mr. Willis, did you become aware of an incident that night?"

"Huh?"

The A.P. dropped his voice to the tone an adult would use on a child, and said, "Did you notice something going on outside?"

"Oh, yeah."

"What did you notice?"

"Some guy got stabbed outside."

Dan couldn't see the prosecutor's expression while he was questioning the witness, but when he turned back to his table and shuffled a few sheets of paper, it read clearly of puzzlement. Something was going on. Dan could feel it, too. Even from a witness who'd rather be somewhere else, answers generally came a good bit easier. The prosecutor turned around to Willis again.

"And," he sighed, "did you, how did you know someone got stabbed outside?"

Willis started to look even more uncomfortable than before. "I was sort of staring out, like, out the window, and I kind of seen it."

The prosecuting attorney took a deep breath, then passed a hand over his tie in a nervous gesture. He took a couple of steps to a point between the jury box and the witness, then asked: "And did you see who it was that got stabbed?"

"Yeah"

"Well, who was it?"

"Harvey Sears."

101

"And, Mr. Willis," he leaned forward, "did you see who stabbed him?"

"No."

"And the man who ... huh? What did you say?" His voice rose up to a soprano screech.

"I said, no, I didn't see who stabbed him."

The prosecutor's jaw dropped open and his eyes bugged out as his face started to turn purple. At the far table, Dan could see the defendant smirk and poke his surprised lawyer in the ribs. As he was turning his attention back, the prosecutor was still gurgling, trying to absorb what he'd just heard and to control himself. He was losing his star witness, the only man who'd actually seen Andrew (AKA: Honeydew) Mellon stab Harvey Sears. He wasn't helped any by the laughter on Mellon's part. The low murmur of the courtroom had exploded into cheers, catcalls and shouting by a group of spectators who appeared to be Mellon's cheering section. The judge started angrily swinging his gavel, trying to force order on an audience intent on disruption.

After getting partial hold on himself, the A.P. managed to gurgle, "Your honor, may we approach the bench?" even as he was lunging to where the judge sat. Dan couldn't hear what was going on, but from the wild arm waving and paper slapping, it was obvious to him that Assistant Prosecutor William Thomas had just been had. Badly. Dan could only catch a little of the conversation, and those parts that he could get consisted of words like "perjury," "intimidation," "setup" and others mostly repetitive of the theme of the conversation.

In the general uproar which the judge and now the bailiff were trying to control, Thomas spun around and leaned over the defendant's table. The hatred in his eyes was evident and made worse by the bland and unconcerned expression on Mellon's face.

Dan strained to hear Thomas. "I'll get you, you son of a bitch," he said. "You're mine. You're scum. And if it's the last thing I ever do, I'll get you. Don't sleep, don't even close your eyes, keep looking over your shoulder, because one day I'll be there, and your ass'll be mine."

Dan mulled the intensity of Thomas' outburst, comparing it to the possibility that Lew had passed on to him. Now it seemed less absurd. Here, clearly, was a man so angry that he could, that he WOULD, kill.

It took Judge Thorley several minutes of gavel-pounding to re-store order to his courtroom, along with multiple threats of con-tempt charges. Eventually he had the quiet he was pounding his gavel for and turned to the defendant's table.

"Mister Mellon," he began, "In my many years upon the bench I have seldom witnessed a scene such as has unrolled itself before me here today. It is quite clear that the State's case has been fa-tally compromised, somehow tampered with, and I intend to have the appropriate office get to the bottom of this ..."

Dan's attention to the judge was interrupted by a bailiff tap-ping him on the shoulder. "They're ready for you, Perkins, come on," he said. As Dan started to stand up, he tuned in to the judge again. "... no choice but to dismiss these charges and adjourn. But I am very confident, young man, that I shall see you in my courtroom again."

Dan was halfway out of his seat, his mind already changing gears and getting ready for his testimony downstairs, so it didn't register as he was pushing his way up the aisle that the little old lady next to him had grimly muttered, "No, you won't, Freddie, no, you won't."

* * * * * * * * *

"So, how did it go?" Lew asked.

"Sort of a draw, I guess. His lawyer was trying to work in some doubt about whether the junk was actually in Lane's possession or just near him. Even tried to infer we planted it, just to make the pop. You?"

"Same thing," Lew answered. "I think he's real close to getting this crumb off." Lew heaved himself up off the bench in the witness room of Division 6. He gathered up his topcoat and handed Dan his. "Well, from here on in, it's not our problem. The prosecutor does his job right, the jury hasn't been tampered with, the judge hasn't been bought, the guy'll get guilty." He punched the DOWN button between the heavily embossed sets of brass elevator doors.

"Then all that has to happen is the judge doesn't decide to do

103

some social experimenting, maybe sentence him to 15 minutes' community service or some other silly shit, and maybe this punk goes away for awhile. But don't hold your breath."

Dan sighed and studied the fake mosaic on the floor. It was done in linoleum squares of varying colors and cuts, a legacy from the original builders of the courthouse, halfway between art deco and WPA. "Yeah, I know, we bring 'em in, they let 'em out. Hey, remind me, we get back to the car, I got another idea."

Lew looked at him, halfway puzzled, but unwilling to ask right then. The elevator had arrived, and they didn't want to talk in front of unknowns. They maintained silence until they pushed through the revolving doors and were out in the cold rain.

As Lew unlocked the right side door, Dan began in a low tone. "You remember telling me that Grimes thought we might want to look inside the department, or maybe inside the court system? The thing about there might be a possible link between all these killings, that each had walked on a major felony?"

"Yeah, I remember," Lew answered.

Dan swung the door, thumped it closed twice before it caught and continued. "Okay, try this. While you were in the courtroom trying to remember your name and doing your best not to embarrass the forces of law and order, I was up in Division 10, observing the workings of justice. I watched two spectacular things."

Lew broke in with a sardonic, "Yeah, who was she?"

"Crude, you peasant, incredibly crude. Try to maintain at least a little dignity. What I watched was, I saw that Mellon dude, you remember, did that homicide back in July? I saw him just beat a rap for murder one. Prosecution witness had a convenient case of bad eyesight. Okay, suddenly we got a possible client. A major felon, who ain't gonna do day one on his rap. Then the next thing I see, is the Assistant Prosecutor, you know, Willy Thomas? Old Law 'n' Order, old Hang 'em High? I watched him totally lose it right there in the courtroom. I swear that man would've, could've, hell, he was GONNA kill Mellon, right there on the spot. He just came apart, my man. Took the judge a hell of a lot of hammering down, the way things were, before he could get any kind of order. Thing about it is, Bro, somebody like that, pissed off like that, at somebody like that, somebody like us ought to look real close at somebody like that."

"Jeez, Dan," Lew flinched, "who writes your stuff? That's the worst sentence I ever heard you say. But it does make sense. Yeah, we get back, let's pull up everything we can get on Mellon, then see what we can get sort of quiet-like on Thomas. Then we see if we can figure out a couple of moves. These guys might just open up the whole thing for us … assuming, of course, that one of our sour apples doesn't do something about it. Goddamn, Dan, before we couldn't even find a suspect, we couldn't so much as buy a lead; now we got too many. We got enough could-be's, we're tripping over them."

"Feast or famine, Bro, chicken or feathers. Hey, steal somebody's parking space so we won't have so far to walk in the freakin' rain."

Later that day, Lew walked back to his desk with a stack of papers half a foot thick in his hands. "You believe this?" he asked. "This's Mellon. These case files go back to when he was 11 freakin' years old, when he was first busted for rolling drunks. Along with these files, the little bastard's got a yellow sheet three full pages' worth. You take your pick, he's got 'em. Felonies, misdemeanors, no-no's, from juvie to Superior Court, he's a walkin' encyclopedia of the damn criminal code."

Dan turned a shocked face upward. "You mean he won't make Eagle Scout? He ain't gonna be choirmaster this year? AAaaaaww."

"Listen, fool, you want Eagle Scout? The odds are he stole the whole troop. Choir? He probably held up the whole congregation some Sunday, then stole the damn bell on the way out. That's as a kid. As an adult, well, this guy holds the patent on bad news. Read."

After a few minutes' skimming, Dan looked across. "Yep, this's definitely a potential customer for the killer. Now, who's the potential killer?"

"That, my man, took just a tad more delicate work. This," he held up a thin folder, "this's the pre-employment background investigation on one William Andrew Thomas, Assistant Prosecuting Attorney, caped crusader, avenger of the outraged public, all-around good guy and potential customer. Incidentally, I don't really have this report. It's still locked safely away in the executive personnel files, secured from the prying eyes of such low-lifes as we. I never saw it, you never saw it. But don't be surprised if that foxy soul honey down in Personnel lays claim to your bod. I had to offer her

105

something during negotiations, and you came to mind."

Dan crashed into the front of his desk as he leaned closer. "You mean, THE fox? You're talking about the honey with the perpetual-motion tush and the legs up to here? You done give this home boy to the African Queen? You may not be too bright, Bro, but I got to give you points for lucky." Dan's hands waved vaguely in front of Lew's forehead as he intoned, "Te absolvo, te absolvo. I forgive you every stupid thing you ever did. You just made up for it all." He looked at the ceiling. "Yeah, God really must love us street cops, after all. Between Ray Salerno's bribe and your bribe ... Hhmmmm. Tell you what, we get done with that file, I don't want you to have to walk all that distance just to return it. That'd be terrible. I'll just put myself out and carry this heavy old file all that way and give it to her myself — sort of see it don't get lost and all. What's in it?"

"You already heard the good news. The bad news is, there's diddly in here that's worthwhile. His education runs through an upper Michigan high school, Columbia University, NYU Law; employment covers mostly hand labor during summer vacations, some clerking during law school, pretty humdrum stuff. Didn't even get busted for anything during spring break. That's assuming he ever went to Lauderdale. What we got here is, we got Jack the Dull Boy. Only fact even vaguely out of the ordinary is that several of the personal references tell of him having a hell of a temper, and his current address is near where that guy got machine-gunned. That ain't hardly worth the cigar, but it's all there is. Want to read it?"

"No, if you've already been through it, there won't be anything new to jump out at me," Dan answered. "Just to be on the safe side, though, how about first thing tomorrow we try to talk Danilovitch into lending us a couple of bodies to do some surveillance? Maybe we'll catch him in a good mood."

Lew looked at his watch. "Tomorrow? Why not today? You see what time it is? We got plenty of time."

"You got time, I don't. This file here has to be safely deposited, back where it came from. You still got my after-shave in your locker?"

Lew held his hand over his heart. "I promise, we'll just go in, tell him what's on our minds, then get the hell out. Never even sit down, if that'll convince you."

"Yeah," Dan said, "I've heard that song before."

Lew's face took on a wounded look. "Dan, you wound me to the quick. Would I lie to you?"

"Bigger 'n' shit, Bro," came the answer. "In a New York minute."

"Okay, I give up, you cynical bastard, we'll talk to him tomorrow."

As they walked into Danilovitch's outer office the next morning, Dan jabbed his partner in the ribs. "I knew it, I just knew it," he said.

The desk in front of Danilovitch's door was once again occupied. This time by a young woman who looked like an escapee from the 11th grade. She was slowly typing something on a brightly colored electric typewriter, while she held the telephone receiver to her right ear with a shoulder. As they approached, they could hear her half of the conversation. "Yeah ... Totally ... Yeah ... Awesome ... Uh, huh ... Yeah ..."

Lew wondered how she could talk and chew gum at the same time with her mouth open, but he let it pass. He wondered instead how two fairly large cops, the only other inhabitants of the office, could be standing in front of her desk without her noticing them.

The conversation went on: "Yeah, well, I never heard her say that, and if he says he heard her say that, well, I don't know where he was, but I was right there, and she never ... uh, yeah ... Totally ..."

Dan and Lew exchanged looks. Dan shrugged, as if to say, "Don't blame me, Bro, I don't do the hiring around here."

Lew shifted his weight from foot to foot, then leaned over, placing his palms on each side of the typewriter, and cleared his throat. Loud. Twice. The conversation went on; the typing stopped; her eyes remained unfocused. Finally, Dan reached out and punched a half-dozen buttons on the touch-tone set.

Slowly, as if coming up from a coma, she refocused her eyes and saw them for the first time. "Hold on a minute. I got somebody," she said to whoever was on the other end, and looked up. "Huh?"

"Is Captain Danilovitch in?" Lew asked.

She turned her head between Dan and Lew. "Huh?"

Dan tried. "Big guy, white shirt, gold badge, lives through that door there, is he in?"

"Huh?"

Lew sighed, "Never mind," and they walked past her. As they were walking through Danilovitch's door, they heard her restart the conversation, again, with whatever entity she was in communion: "Uh, yeah, I'm back ... yeah ..."

Clearly the Captain wasn't in a good mood. He was correcting the spelling of a typed letter on his desk, carefully lettering each word above the incorrectly spelled one. His opening words were, "Either of you guys know how to type?"

Dan and Lew simultaneously pointed at each other. "He does," they echoed.

"You see what I got out there? Why are they doing this to me? What've I ever done to the Civil Service Board? What'd I ever do to deserve this in the first place?"

Lew shrugged. I don't know, Captain, maybe it's bad karma, or something. You believe in a previous life? Maybe you did something to Shirley MacLaine in a previous life, and now she's getting even. Who knows?"

"Yeah, well, either way, it's my problem. What'd you want to see me about?"

Dan led off. "We got maybe an idea, Captain, we'd like to try it out, see what you think ..."

Twenty minutes later, two fairly large cops walked out of the Captain's office and became as invisible as the purple-faced uniformed sergeant who was awaiting recognition by the temporary occupant of the secretary's chair. They thumbed him through the door and walked on. As they gently closed the outer door behind them, the last thing they heard was, "Yeah ... Totally ... Awesome ..."

* * * * * * * * *

With a hand full of mail and his key in the other hand, Dan paused just inside his apartment door. "Okay, Tigger Cat, jump," he said. And Tigger Cat jumped from atop the bookcase next to the doorway onto his right shoulder. A rub of whiskers against his jaw, and Tigger settled down for the ride into the bedroom. This routine had gone on for almost two years, ever since he'd picked up a stray kitten one day early in his partnership with Lew. If you'd asked him, he would never admit to collecting strays, of whatever persuasion.

He walked into the bedroom, dumped Tigger, hung his jacket in the closet and then unhooked the holster from his belt and laid the piece next to it. It was a gun older than most of the cops that he knew. Not many people carried the old Colt .38 Police Positive any more. Everyone else, it seemed, opted for Glocks .40's, .41's, .357's, magnum hot loads, armor-piercing crap. Hell, he suspected there were a few out there who'd love to get their hands on tracer ammunition if they could.

The gun was a legacy from his father, who'd taught him to shoot almost as soon as his boyish hands were capable of holding the gun. His father's training had been excellent; under different circumstances he might have been a nationally ranked competitor. The disease that killed him, though, had first taken away his ability to control his muscles, and with it his ability to remain a cop. He'd died more slowly than if he'd been cut down in the streets of his native Detroit which, Dan believed, he'd rather have had happen to him. But it hadn't been that way, and nothing Dan could do would bring things back the way they were. Things change. Nothing is forever; Dan knew and accepted that. But he could maintain some connection with the past by carrying his father's service revolver. Little gun or not, it was all he needed anyway.

His father's advice had been, "If you're good enough, you can do it with a .22. If you're not good enough, an automatic cannon won't help you. Mostly, though, try to talk. A bullet's too permanent, and you can't ever call it back. If you're gonna be a cop, your job's to help, not hurt."

Dan walked into the kitchen, pulled a beer from the refrigerator and sat down at the kitchen table. He rifled through the mail, separating the wonderful offers he couldn't live without and the millions of dollars he might have already won from the real mail. That left three pieces. An electric bill, his Mastercharge bill and a letter from Detroit in his mother's handwriting.

"Sorry, Ma, this I'll read tomorrow," he said. "Tonight, I have sinful things on my mind with the African Queen."

The letter waited on the table as he walked back into the bedroom, laid out some fresh clothing and cranked up the shower. This would be no ordinary date. The African Queen was known for stunning good looks and devastating wit. It was said that she didn't do cops. He'd never gotten so much as a tumble from her but, oddly enough, good old humdrum Lew, in his direct and unsophisticated approach, had charmed her out of the file and into meeting Dan.

Their initial superficial conversation had been the usual patter, but when she mentioned that she was going to law school three nights a week, Dan saw something more serious in her than he'd initially supposed. His point of view changed, and with it, his approach. This was some kind of classy lady, worthy of his sincere efforts. "Tigger," he said, "tonight we meet us a real lady. Wish me luck."

Chapter 12

IN the bad old days of Chicago, when the Mafiosi were applying Darwin's Law to gangdom, there came about a very efficient means of removing competitors from the scene. A selected hit man would catch his potential trophy off guard, preferably at a restaurant or in a barbershop, walk in, blow him away and then walk out. That was all there was to it. It was done in almost as little time as it takes to tell, and if done quickly enough, nobody made it a point to come up from under the table long enough to look, much less identify the killer.

That particular means of organizational outplacement and competitive one-upsmanship still exists today. So it was no particular surprise to the Police Department that three semi-independent locals, Lugo "Bad Fat" Spinelli, Gerolamo "The Chipmunk" Scalisi, and another minor, but also three-first-named hood were removed from the criminal hierarchy of the city. What did come as a surprise, though, was the existence of sufficient physical evidence, in the form of a dropped key ring and one partial fingerprint, to obtain an indictment. And indict they did. Over the course of the investigation the Homicide boys had worked overtime for three weeks, augmented a few bodies from the Uniforms and rousted half the city's hoods. They finally managed to zero in on one Salvatore "The Squid" Matula, a button man for the Della Romagna family. Allegedly, of course.

The trial lasted slightly over three days. Salvatore walked out a free man, after his attorney impeached the testimony of the investigating officers concerning how they traced the key ring to Salvatore's front door, poked huge procedural holes in the constitutionality of the investigation and managed to convince the jury that the partial fingerprint could've been anybody's coming in the restaurant, in spite of it having enough points of identification to tie it specifically to him. In short, the lawyer was good, the evidence wasn't, and the suspicion existed that more than one member of the jury saw his best interests in letting Salvatore out on the street again.

Which courtesy Salvatore appreciated. Ordinarily, that would have been the end of it, except that on a frosty Halloween, Salvatore was eating linguini at Piazza Roma, when he was unceremoniously removed from the administrative rolls of his family. In keeping with long-standing local tradition, nobody saw anything. Well, almost nobody. Mr. Dieter Gustafson, from Duluth, Minnesota, also happened to be present. Not being a local in tune with the delicacy of these matters, he observed and duly disclosed to the police what he'd seen. Not that it was a whole lot of help.

Lew and Dan had been called out on this one in the clear suspicion that this might be the vigilante killer again. They worked the crime scene, checked the evidence or lack of it with the lab men, requested a series of photographs and then got down to interviewing Mr. Gustafson. Who wasn't all that much help.

"What I saw was, I'm pretty sure it was a man, wearing a long overcoat and one of those old-guy head masks. You know, the kind the kids wear them on Halloween. It fits over your head, and it's like, it's an old man's face, with a mostly bald head, with a little fringe of hair around the sides, you know? You look out the eye-holes. I had one for a party once, it was a gorilla mask like that, and you can't wear 'em for very long. You start to sweat inside, because there's not enough room in the nostril holes for you to breath out of, you know? For the rest, I'd guess he was maybe five-six, one-fifty, one-sixty, not very big, is what I mean, I guess."

Dan looked up from the notes he was writing. "Mister Gustafson, what did you see of it? How did this go down?"

"Go down?"

"Yes, I mean, how did it happen? What exactly did you see?"

Gustafson murmured "how it went down" to himself a couple of times, as if he planned to use the phrase back home when he told the story. "Well, how it went down was," he grinned a satisfied grin as if he'd just learned a new card trick, "I'm sitting over there when it went down," he pointed, "with my back to the door, like, and I just happen to look up as this guy is coming past my table. He's like five feet or so away from me, so that's how I know he's got this mask on, I can see it as he goes by. Then he walks up to the last table there where the dead guy's eating, and I'm looking back toward him, on account of the mask gets my attention, and I'm wondering why Trick or Treat in a restaurant downtown, and I hear these two soft pops, not real loud at all. And then he goes out the back door there, I guess, into the kitchen. The dead guy doesn't fall over right away, like on TV, you know? So it's a couple of more seconds before I understand what went down. That's about all I know. I hope it helps you."

Lew refocused his eyes from the rear of the room where the Medical Examiner's men were removing the body. Gustafson followed his gaze intently, turning halfway to his left.

"What color coat, Mr. Gustafson?"

"Blue. With white, like plaid stripes."

"How'd you see that? Was the raincoat open?"

"Oh, the other guy. I thought you meant what the dead guy's wearing."

Lew sighed. It had already been one of those days. His ex's lawyer was after him for more alimony, the power steering gave out on his car, the sole of his shoe was coming loose, and now he had a witness with a case of terminal dumb.

"No, sir, I meant the suspect. I don't need you to describe the victim. He's not going anywhere."

Gustafson turned back to Lew, unfazed.

"Oh, yeah. I see what you mean."

"Okay," Lew tried again. "What color coat was the suspect wearing?"

"It was a light brown, sort of a camel's hair color."

"And, which hand did he hold the gun in, sir?"

"The right, I think."

"And the shoes, the pants, what color were they?"

"I don't know; I didn't notice."

"All right, sir," Lew continued, "we'll need to get a written statement from you before you go home, and we'd appreciate it if you'd let us know if there's anything else comes to mind that you haven't told us yet. It may not seem important, but tell us anyway, if you would."

"Yeah, sure," Gustafson answered. "Does that mean you're done with me now?"

"Yessir, have a good night. We'll contact you at your hotel in the morning to set up an appointment to come in and give your statement."

As Gustafson walked out the door, Dan softly pounded his fist on the table. "Goddamn it, Lew, this's obviously one of ours. And the sonofabitch is laughing at us. He just knocks off a Mafia hard guy clean as you please, does it professionally and then just disappears. Granted it could've been one of the crime families to have done this, but it's our boy. I just know it is."

Lew picked a breadstick off the table and started to munch. "Yeah, this guy may be laughing, but we rate at least a smile. You caught the description Gustafson gave us, that takes Canby out of the running. He's six-foot-two, weighs about two-ten. No way he'd be able to pass for the guy did this." He held up the stub of a breadstick for emphasis. "We reduced the number of possibles by one. It can't be Canby."

Dan smiled. "I don't believe you said that. 'Can't be Canby'? Don't you ever bitch about my turn of phrase, ever again, Bro. And if you're through feeding your face, let's make like cops again."

Lew moved away from the table, holding another breadstick in his hand. "I like the garlic ones. Helps keep away the vampires."

As the activity of the crime scene wound down, Lew and Dan headed out the door to their car.

"Look at the friggin' jackals, standing around out here to catch a sight of blood. Hell, I'll bet for the next two months you'll have to fight your way in here to have dinner. Place'll be the current hot spot with the hip crowd. Just look at them."

Lew poked his partner and nodded his head as he stuffed his hands in his coat pockets. "Check that one out, Dan, the old guy in the tan topcoat. Right height, right weight. Pity he's got most of his hair, but he must be 90. He'd work out good as a suspect."

Dan answered, "Yeah, let's go roust him, see if a cannon falls out of his pockets. Come to think of it, I read somewhere that the population of the country over 65 is growing. More old people living longer, better medicine, that kind of thing. It's supposed to be why Social Security's going broke. Can't afford all the survivors. You know," he mused, "maybe they're right, too. Every place I go, it sure seems like there's a lot of old people hanging around. Well, what the hell, they got nothing else to do, let 'em. Me, when I get that old, it's off to Saint Pete, pushing shuffleboards, or whatever."

Lew's attention was split between what his partner was saying and the traffic he was maneuvering through. "Yeah," he agreed, "lots of old people, everywhere you go."

The next day, several conversations were going on in several places downtown. One of them went like this:

"Well, what have you got for me?"

"Nothing."

"Don't hand me that shit. What do you think I pay you for, just because I like you? What the hell's going on down there?"

"I'm telling you the truth, we just don't know. We got two of our better people working on it. They've been all over a whole rash of them, and there's nothing there. We just don't know."

"You just don't know," the seated man mimicked. "Okay, wise guy, here's something I know. I don't give a shit about a whole rash of killings, I'm only interested in one. One, you understand? Somebody took one of my soldiers out. Somebody took out ONE OF MY HOUSE! You understand that, ONE OF MY HOUSE was took out. I can't let that go past. Nobody, nobody ever takes out one of your house, without either sanction from the commission, or he wants to start off a war. You find out who it is. If it's a move on me, I want to know. If it was a sanctioned whack, I'd know about it long before now. So whatever it is, you find out. Quick. Otherwise, I don't want to be you. Do you understand that?" The speaker lapsed into a variety of Sicilian dialect very rarely heard in this part of the country. "Du gabizhe?"

The answer was as rarely heard. "U gabizhu. I understand."

"Good. Now get out of here, same way you came in." And a police lieutenant of long standing and honorable service in the force left the home offices of a major real estate investment company and took the elevator nine floors down to the basement, where he walked out through a back door into an alley.

Three days later, Lew and Dan received a preliminary report

from the forensic lab downstairs. Since it was signed by Leo Coppoldi, they were inclined to accept it as a final report, as an unchangeable report, as complete and accurate as it could ever be. Coppoldi's background in criminalistics (which is the proper word; criminology is the study of criminals) went back through the work of a Swedish physicist named Soderman, who wrote on the subject in the early 40s, all the way back to Eugene Vidocq, a Frenchman regarded as the father of the subject, who wrote the first definitive work back in the 1800s. Coppoldi had read virtually everything published since then and had written a lot of it himself. If Coppoldi told you something, you accepted it. Coppoldi KNEW. And this time around, Coppoldi knew that the bullets removed from the head of the late Salvatore Matula and the brass recovered at the scene were Remington hollow-point .22 longs fired from a Colt Woodsman. Also included in the report was the fact that the Colt Woodsman hadn't been manufactured for many years, Mafia hit men used to favor it, and the bullets had been fired from 3.5 to 5.0 feet away.

After reading the report, Lew handed it across to Dan. Dan read it through to the end, then pitched it into the tray holding the folders. "Let me tell you, my man, this sucks. There's somebody out there, he's doing these guys, and he's one class act. Wouldn't surprise me if he's getting a real chuckle out of jumping us through all these hoops." His voice dropped so as to just carry across the desk. "Tell you the truth, Lew, I'm not too sure this bastard might not really be too good for us."

"Uh, uh, pal," Lew said without lifting his gaze from the desktop. "Us, we can make a thousand mistakes, doing our job, we'll eventually get it right once. Him, he can't make even one. Whoever he is, however good he is, he's only human. And that means that sooner or later, he's gonna make a mistake. And when he does make that mistake, you and I'll be standing there waiting for him. No problem, Dan, he's ours; it may take just a little longer than we'd like, but he is ours."

Dan stretched, got out of his chair and started to put on his coat. "Yeah, you're right; it's just that sometimes it seems like such a damn losing battle. There's more of them than there is of us; they pull something, we chase after them, somebody else pulls something, we go chase after them too, roundy-round, don't never end.

116

How's about lunch? I'll stick you with the chcck. That'll make me feel better, then we'll go catch up with a few snitches, maybe hear a little something."

As Lew pulled himself out of the chair, he answered, "Why the hell not? I've bought you enough meals to take you on as a damn dependent anyway. Cobo's do it?"

"Yeah, that'll be fine. We sort of need to be back here no later than five, all right? No overtime today. Got to meet a very special lady."

"Damn," Lew answered, "that eases my fears. All this time you've been spending down in Personnel, I thought you were looking for a regular job with the city."

"Naw, not me, man, I've been a cop long enough, I'm no longer suited for an honest job." Lew grabbed the keys off the desktop. "I'll drive. If I have to pay for lunch, you get to rassle with the freakin' passenger door."

* * * * * * * * * *

Later that evening, Lew parked on a picturesque street lined with trees whose thin tops ended at about 15 feet, had the spindly trunks often found on greenhouse rush-grown products and were held vertical by a series of guy wires. He looked up and down the street at the picturesque refurbished brick buildings, spat on the picturesque brick sidewalk and walked to the non-picturesque sedan parked a hundred picturesque feet away. It was obviously an unmarked unit, since it was plain, American-made, had four doors, no whitewalls and an extra antenna. Lew opened the passenger door and slid in, thankful that at least the interior light switch had been disabled.

"You got any idea how badly these wheels stand out from the rest on this street?"

Sid Loman put a Styrofoam cup of coffee on the dash, then belched. "Goddamn, I got to quit meatball sandwiches. Talk about unrequited love, how can I love something that hates me so bad? Don't blame me for the wheels, Lew. I asked, I begged, I pleaded for a 300-ZX, said I'd settle for any European piece of shit, I'd even go for a Trans-Am. You know what they told me? They said this's just a homicide, use what we got. Fancy cars're only for big stuff like major drug cases. You think Miami Vice'd put up with this shit?"

Loman belched again. "No action on your boy. He went out around 7, cruised a few singles bars, came home alone at 10:42, through the door. Lights're still on; from the flickers of light I get now and then, he's watching TV in the front room there. You wanna take over for a while or what?"

"No, Sid, you've got it, just knock off when you've put him to bed for sure." Lew started to ease out the door. "I don't know how long we're going to be doing this; I appreciate your help, man."

Sid reached down beside him and started to unwrap another meatball sandwich. "Don't thank me, this's all overtime and gravy to boot. Long as the Captain okays my overtime chit, this's just fine with me. I can use the money. Besides," he continued, talking around his sandwich, "it keeps me the hell outa the house. You know what I mean?"

"Yeah," Lew said, as he started to press the door shut, "well, it helps a lot. See you tomorrow, Sid."

The next morning Lew put down his coffee, slipped off his sport jacket and opened the manila envelope on his desk. He had to cut through the transparent tape that held the flap closed. Inside he found a neatly typed, although short, surveillance report. After glancing across the administrative data at the top, he dropped to the "Synopsis" section and began to read:

"Visual surveillance of SUBJECT acquired at 1753 hours, as SUBJECT departed place of employment, Hall of Justice. SUBJECT observed to proceed directly to residence, arriving at 1822 hours, in own vehicle, previously identified. SUBJECT departed residence at 1901 hours, using own vehicle. SUBJECT observed at three cocktail lounges (see Details section), returned alone to residence at 2242 hours. No further extra-residence activity. SUBJECT's interior lights extinguished at 2347 hours, no further activity observed. Surveillance terminated at 0030 hours."

Lew looked down at the yellow square notepaper stuck to the bottom of the sheet, and read:

"Lew — I make it eight hours O'time, counting report write-up. Will pick up again tonight, unless you say not to.

— *Sid*"

From over his shoulder Dan grunted. "Huh. That don't help us a whole lot, Bro."

"No, it doesn't," Lew answered soberly. "But it's the best we can get for a while until we come up with something better. If Thomas is our boy, we need to hope for him to do something overt, I don't know what, go stalking bad guys or something. The Captain's juggling the budget to cover for the overtime, but we're going to have to carry the major load ourselves on this. I'd give a lot to be able to get inside his apartment and see if he's got any guns."

Dan snickered, "Yeah, sure, Bro. What have you got, some kind of death wish or something? You really want to go jack with an Assistant Prosecutor's rights? Sheeit, man, he'd have you for breakfast. Your unemployed ass'd owe him damages from now till forever. You either catch him dirty, or you don't catch him at all."

"Just a thought, Dan, just a thought."

"Don't think, man, it makes the top of your head melt."

"This for you," Lew said, as he filed the report neatly away in the folder.

Chapter 13

As they entered the captain's sanctum sanctorum, Dan nudged his partner, whose head was turned toward the door he was closing. At the nudge, Lew turned, refocused his eyes and saw the emaciated corpse of a starvation victim whose embalmer had failed basic makeup. The corpse was propped up in the secretary's chair, wearing a bright red shoulder-length wig, pale blue eye shadow applied to its leathery brown face with a pallet knife, pale pink lipstick not quite on straight, and a purple flowered blouse. On its dehydrated arms were hung a dozen yellow plastic hoops. The corpse's head was rolled forward on its bony chest, and some joker with a macabre sense of humor had placed a lighted cigarette in its mouth. It took a second for Lew to recognize the sound he heard as the high-pitched roar of an electric typewriter being stressed to its limits, and to accept that the corpse had just exhaled a solid cloud of smoke. The apparition looked up without pausing in its typing and said, "Good morning, gentlemen, can I help you?"

"Uh, yes, ma'am, Detectives Perkins and Perkins, uh, to see, uh, the Captain," Lew said, still trying to absorb the scene.

"Go right in, gentlemen, he had me call you just a minute ago, but you'd already left." The roar continued.

As they walked past her desk, Dan bounced a little in his step and mumbled, "Lookin' good, Mama."

The cold stare of death warmed a little as she answered, "Yo, Bro," and dropped her head again.

Once past her desk, Lew paused, then quickly turned around to look over her shoulder at the page in the typewriter. Instead of the random strings of unrelated letters he'd expected, he saw neat paragraphs of what, from the few words he could quickly scan, was a budget report. He quick-stepped to catch up, his mind still trying to digest what he'd seen.

As they stepped though the doorway, Danilovitch looked up. "Damn fast, I'll give you that. She couldn't have called over there more than two minutes ago."

Dan deadpanned, "We ran when we heard it was you, Captain."

"Yeah, sure. I hope you guys have some good news for me, 'cause the shit just hit the fan." He flipped around a newspaper he'd been reading and pointed to a column on the right edge of the page. From the location Dan knew it was "The View From Here," a column written daily by Jerry Here, who was never happy about anything. As he read, he reflected that this column wasn't much of a change.

"This reporter doesn't much care for garbage in the streets. I'm not too particular about whether it's the sacked kind, which our esteemed Sanitation Department (now, there's a misnomer) occasionally picks about 50% of up, or the two-legged kind, which our courts consistently turn loose after those rare occasions when our Police Department reluctantly picks one or two of them up. Having said that, dear readers, let me point out that our not-so-fair city has more than its share of both, and now, apparently, is getting an even more vicious brand of the two-legged kind. I'd like to point out that in the last few months we've been treated to a crime wave that would make Al Capone's Chicago seem like a Smurf's convention, by comparison. Bodies are, quite literally, littering the streets like leftovers from a World War II movie, and our Police Department won't or can't do anything about it. For the past four that I know about, and quite possibly more months, at a rate of around one a week, people are getting shot, knifed, in one case arrowed, possibly electrocuted, and who knows? maybe carcompacted to death, while our flatfoots walk their beats, or more accurately, ride in air-conditioned splendor, nailing jaywalkers, spitters-on-the streets, violators of the unlicensed garage-sale ordinances, and ladies of the evening. Where are they when there's killing going on? Why, there they are, busting little old ladies at garage sales, enforcing traffic laws and gener-

ally saving the world from the likes of such lawbreakers, that's where they are. Where they AIN'T, my friends, is out where the bullets, knives, arrows, yes, even maybe car-compactors are flying. They're not there when it's happening, and they're surely not there before it's happened, which would certainly ease the need for fire-hydrant water to wash all the blood away. How about it, boys? Shall we quit busting the little guys, and start going for the bigger fish? Do you really mean to tell me that some gang is knocking off another gang, for surely it HAS to be a gang takeover — oh, by the way, did I mention that all these killings are of people KNOWN to the cops? Yes, I said KNOWN. They aren't just random good citizens, knocked off by irate husbands, wives, burglars, etc., they're what we used to call, in gentler days, POLICE CHARACTERS. Yeah, that's right, not an anonymous one in the bunch, and these esteemed minions of the law, these protectors of civilization, these upholders of justice, whose purpose it is to protect and to serve, yeah, all that, either don't know how or don't care to stop it. Come to think of it, maybe it shouldn't stop for a while. Maybe the solution is to let them kill one another off, until there's only one left. Then the cops can pick up the sole survivor, turn him over to the courts to either set loose or send to some country-club prison somewhere, and go back to sleep. Unless they wake up to bust some more little old ladies holding unlicensed garage sales. That's the view from here. Tomorrow, we'll look at what the building inspectors REALLY do with your tax money."

Dan whistled, and handed the paper to Lew. "Pretty strong stuff," he commented. "Reads like he's really got one on for us this time."

"He does, he does indeed," Danilovitch confirmed. "He's pissed because his mother got a summons for running a week-long garage sale, without a permit yet. Somebody reported her, so it costs her 15 bucks. Now he's gonna get 15 bucks' worth of our hides out of it. Talk about Murphy's Law, he came down to get the ticket fixed, couldn't, got pissed off, and then got lucky. Somebody's loose mouth got him interested, and he dug into it."

"Well," Lew said, "at least he doesn't know how far into the woods we actually are on this, or he'd really have us for breakfast."

Danilovitch squirmed uncomfortably in his chair. "I take it that means you still haven't got anything for me on this?"

"Sorry, Captain," Dan threw in, "we're doing the best we can, but there just isn't anything to work with. Hell, so far the best we came up with is maybe a wild-assed D.A., trying to make street justice. And even that's pretty thin, but it's somebody who'd have access to court records, proceedings and such. You remember we briefed you on the possible tie-in? All these guys walked recently on major felonies. But that's all we got. So far surveillance hasn't given us anything, and unless he makes some sort of overt move, all we can do is wait and watch."

"You zeroing in on that, or are you still looking at other possibilities? I don't want you to get a case of tunnel vision on this thing."

"Nope," Dan answered, "we're still playing the whole game. We thought we had something with the little guy and the Dirty Harry piece, but that fell apart, right there in your office."

"Come to think of it, hindsight being 20-20 and all that, the little guy, whatsizname? He wouldn't have worked out anyway. He wouldn't have had the access to court records, or to our own files. That's got to be key on this one." Dan's gaze moved out the window, refocused on the courthouse on the next block. "Means, motive and opportunity. Seems like nobody's got all three....." He shifted his weight then and leaned against the window frame. "Somebody's out there, he's laughing at us, and he's awful good. He's sophisticated enough to make his moves and be gone, like some ... hell, I don't know, but he's pro quality, I'll give him that. I'll sure as hell give him that."

Danilovitch sat there looking unhappy. "I'm taking a lot of heat on this thing. That story's just going to increase the temperature. We need answers, and we need them fast. What can we do to help? You need more help, more facilities, what?"

"We need a damn crystal ball, Captain, is what we need. Either that, or we need nobody gets to beat the rap anymore. Seems like it's open season on rap-beaters," Dan said. "We're still not completely done with the theories that it's either somebody in the court system, or somebody here in our house that's doing it. We started with Canby, Fairfield and Camacho to look at. Canby wasn't right for that restaurant kill. Didn't fit the physical. Besides, we established that he was on duty that night. Maybe a friend of his, if you want to stretch a guess, but I'm pretty sure he's out. That leaves Fairfield and Camacho. We don't know how that'll work, but it's a thing we can't ignore.

"So we look at Thomas. He's got motive, he's got means, maybe he's just enough of a flake to go over the edge. I dunno. Shit, maybe anything. Right about now, hell, Little Red Ridin' Hood looks good for this. But maybe he's clean. If he is, then maybe we need to go through the court system looking at individual cases, see if we can get some correlation between any other people who lost a felony case against some of these hoods got downed. After that, I don't know, we'll just have to hope for inspiration."

"Well, you'd better get it pretty damn quick, gentlemen, damn quick indeed." Danilovitch stood up and turned to a side table, where he picked up a bottle of Pepto-Bismol and took a swallow. In a softer tone of voice, he continued to speak. "Okay, I guess that's it; get me some results, boys, before all our peckers wind up on the anvil."

Chapter 14

LOUIE Hinson stood with his back to the recessed wooden fence that closed the rear exit of the alley, a large black leather-bound Bible resting on his upraised left hand. His ministerial collar was crooked, belying the peace and calm in his face. He should have been cowering. He should have been begging for them not to hurt him, to leave him alone, maybe even offering to let them have all his money. But he definitely shouldn't have been standing there against the fence, and especially not looking so calm.

It was all wrong, and, if they'd been listening a little closer, they might have realized also that what Louie was saying, quite clearly, quite slowly, was also wrong. But what the hell, when you're in a hurry to get the old man's money and get around the block to where the crack house is, you sometimes overlook small details. Which is why they just dismissed the sounds coming from the old reverend, and just assumed they were prayers and let it go at that. So Louie spoke on, as his right hand opened the book, and lay on top of the opened pages.

"And lo, the oppressed and the beaten shall find strength within the Word, and they shall, yea, even evermore, render themselves up to the aid of their Deliverer, who shall have within him a Judge, and, yea, that judge shall have as his servants six statutes of the law, from whom there shall not be appeal. And, yea, those statutes of the law shall belch fire and iron; yea, even evermore, they shall ..."

Zoomer Lane and his cousin Little Willie moved in a little closer, still hearing, but not understanding the preacher's words. After all, they'd stalked this old guy for three blocks before he made the mistake of getting trapped in this alley-mouth, and they were real close now to getting the money and being gone. Willie scanned the street once more, satisfied that no one was in view.

"And yea, the oppressed shall become the oppressors, and even smiting the evil ones hip and thigh, and they shall ..." closer, now, he looked directly at them, they were within ten feet ... "Whereof, he shall say unto them ...," now five feet, "... and he shall say," the voice dropped to a whisper, "So long, scum." And then it was too late.

The old preacher's right hand lifted a loaded and cocked GI .45 automatic from the hollowed Bible. If Zoomer and Willie had cared to look, they would have noticed that it hadn't been a Bible after all. It was a dictionary, with all the pages after "audio-auric" glued together and carved out to leave a large hollow. If they'd cared to notice, they would have noticed that the black leather book itself was a phony, its black leather actually a coat of gloss black (Wal-Mart's, on special at 99 cents,) and the gilt edges also sprayed on with gold paint (also Wal-Mart's) for effect.

But Zoomer and Willie didn't care. Besides, it was too dark to have clearly seen these little details, and they only showed up well in the muzzle flash that illuminated the scene for Willie while Zoomer was taking a bullet in the chest. The second bullet struck Willie slightly off the midline of his body, which is to say slightly into his right lung, which is also to say, not exactly where Louie had been coached on where to aim.

Howard had been very specific about that: "It's a big gun, it's got a heavy recoil, and if your grip's at all wrong, it'll try to get away from you. So your safest shot is up close and straight down the middle. Aim for his belt buckle, you'll hit him in the chest. Get fancy and go for his heart, and you'll likely put it over his shoulder. Don't treat this lightly. Shoot once per man, make your kill clean and close up, and get out of there. Now, do you take cream with your coffee or non-dairy? We've got both of them down here."

The flash of the entire scene ran through Louie's mind at the speed of the bullets themselves. Howard, standing there at his right wearing his old army sweater, pouring out coffee and dispensing shooting tips; the mattresses carefully stacked along the walls and hanging from the basement ceiling to deaden the sounds of the shots; the elaborately rigged baffles and mattresses, constructed to catch the bullets; even the uncomfortable earmuff-style ear protectors which they wore to protect their already-failing hearing. And the smell of burnt cordite, something in it reminiscent of the smokehouse Louie had worked in as a child. It all came back to him in the time it took for Willie to fly backward about six feet and crumple to the cement. He hadn't actually liked the shot, but Willie wasn't moving, and there wasn't any time to think out something else to do, so he continued with the plan.

He put the gun back into the book, checked both ways for witnesses, which in this neighborhood he knew wouldn't likely be a problem, and started to walk away. His black suit and hat blended him into the evening's shadows, and his worn ebony skin helped him into invisibility. Louie Hinson left no trace behind him. None, that is, unless you count one dead Zoomer (formerly known as Cyril) Lane, one dying William Joseph Lane, and two small pieces of brass, cylindrical in shape, nestled in a deep crack in the concrete floor of the alley.

Three blocks, 12 minutes and a whole world away, Sisters Alethea Louise Washington and Charity Grace Robertson walked down the tree-covered sidewalk en route to Thursday Worship and the Bible Fellowship hour afterward. The preacher walking down the sidewalk toward them didn't look familiar, but as he got close enough, he tipped his hat to them. In a manner both courtly and almost roguish, he said, "Ah, good evening, sisters, this's a lovely evening to be doin' the Lord's work, isn't it?"

For the next hundred yards, neither Sister Alethea nor Sister Charity could have gotten into Heaven with what they were thinking.

* * * * * * * * *

The noise in the squadroom had settled down to the usual dull roar by ten-thirty, what with various and sundry miscreants, victims, lawyers, politicos, news writers, news inventors and a lot of cops going about their daily activities. Basically, it was pretty simple; if you were a bad guy, you did something to the neutral guys, which made the good guys bring you in, unless you had a partially good guy to spring you through the exertion of his influence, or a partially bad guy to spring you through his knowledge of where the system didn't always work. And, of course, there were the pure and holy class of guys, who wrote in the newspaper or emoted on-camera about how horrible it was that the oppressive government of these here United States caused the poverty and ignorance which made ... no, more like FORCED, the poor victims of that poverty and ignorance to do things which got them into trouble with the guys who called themselves good guys, but who were actually bad guys, because they represented the system which made all the other formerly good guys into bad guys. Simple, huh?

It was into this peaceful, monastic, yea, even idyllic environment that a good guy who looked more like a bad guy than any of the other bad guys entered. You could tell he was a good guy because his weapon was holstered, he had a gold police badge hung on a metal chain around his neck, there was a photo-identification badge clipped to his belt, and three other good guys murmured pleasantries at him as he threaded his way through the squadroom toward the desks where Lew and Dan sat.

"Scavuzzo, what the hell's this? What happened to the altar boy used to own that badge?" Lew asked, as he looked up at the grungy apparition before him. "You look worse than if you'd took up residence in some sewer, man, and you don't smell none too beautiful either. Get away, man, you give garbage a bad name."

Detective 3rd Anthony Scavuzzo grinned from behind a three-week growth of beard. "You're just jealous, 'cause you can't look as casually elegant as I can. It's just that you're not into the informal look. Besides, the undercover's over as of this morning. Last night we popped 32 assorted thieves, burglars, middle-man fences and one city councilman's brother, who just happened to be passing by and figured to use the men's room or something. Dumb bastard's just standing there, we tell him he's busted, to put down the VCR. He says, "What VCR?" This guy's the best laugh we've had all damn night. Anyway, a good operation. It worked slick, my man, and the D.A.'s grinning from here to here. Says every one's a good pop. But that's not why I'm wasting my time with you two. I got this report for you from the lab. I was down there on some filed-off serial numbers, and they asked me to give this to you quick. Maybe a piece for your vigilante thing?"

"Damn sure hope so," Dan scowled, "so far we're batting zero.

Last night didn't help us one bit at all, either with the mayor, the chief or with anybody else. There's some sonofabitch out there running around, he's offing people right and left, and we don't have the faintest line on what the hell's going down."

Lew added, "Sometimes, hell, nothing goes right. Last night two more bad-asses got it. One of them wasn't quite dead when we got there. The paramedics're keeping him alive with oxygen and plasma, or whatever the hell it is they pump in, and we ask him who did it, you know, try to get something out of him, and all the hell he wants is a preacher. Not just any one, either. Turns out the little bastard's a racist. Get this: the little bastard kept asking for a nigger preacher. Well, hell, I guess he just didn't want to go without making his peace first." Lew stretched, yawned, then held out his hand. "Okay, you've had your look at the elite, now gimme the envelope before somebody in here busts you for felony filthy."

Scavuzzo pitched the envelope on Lew's desk. "Like I said before, jealousy is all." He turned to Dan and recited: "Sticks and stones may break my bones, but whips and chains excite me." He walked away from the two desks, then thought better of it and came back. His face took on a serious expression, as he said, "Whoa. If this's a major break on your vigilante thing, I'm not about to walk away from it without knowing. Open the envelope, let's see what the lab's got for you."

Lew stripped off the tape sealing the envelope and removed several sheets of paper and a small plastic bag marked with several sets of initials, dates and identification numbers. Inside the bag were five expended .45 caliber shells, each individually bagged to keep them from scratching each other. He went to the last page of the report, scanning for the signature. When he recognized that it said, "L. Coppoldi," his confidence level in what he was about to read climbed. Everyone knew that Coppoldi didn't miss. In fact, it was common knowledge that each year the FBI sent him an offer, upping the ante each year, and that each year Coppoldi turned them down.

He scanned the report, his face cracking into a wider and wider grin, until he reached the end. "Bingo," he said, pitching the sheet to his partner. "For a change, we get to score some points. We got a match between these brass from last night and that park killing in the summer. They tie in. Same gun did all five of these dudes." He turned back to Scavuzzo and with a bored and very blase tone of voice, said, "And now, my dear Watson, it becomes very simple indeed. I merely send my apprentice here into the masses, to find out who has that gun, and I shall have apprehended my villain. All rawther simple, don'tcha know."

"Apprentice, your ass," Dan scowled.

Lew held the bags up at eye level, squinting into them with all the intensity of a Gypsy fortune teller trying to tell his own fortune. "These little beauties can't talk yet, my man, but they sure as hell will, someday soon. You wanna know what I think? I think our boy's just about run through his arsenal, and from now on we're looking at matches. I think every bad guy he does now, it's gonna be a match from a previous killing. He slipped up, Dan, and now he's ours."

Dan's voice echoed out from behind a paper cup of coffee. "Not ours, Bro, mine. If you're a good boy, though, I may let you be with me when I nail him."

"Bullshit," Lew retorted. "You couldn't nail a picture to a wall without help. If you're sober enough to walk without embarrassing me, let's hotfoot over to the Captain's office. This he'll want to know about."

Dan had opened his mouth, about to say something, when the phone interrupted him. He picked up the instrument and spoke into it, still half-standing. "Perkins. No, Dan. Yeah, he's here. Yeah. Yeah. Okay, we're just on our way over anyway." He put the phone down. "Lew, that's Danilovitch's secretary. Wants to see us. Now."

Scavuzzo smiled. "So it's lookin' good, huh? Maybe you'll tip me extra for the service?" Lew turned, still moving toward the squadroom door. "You want a tip? I'll give you a tip. Buy low, sell high!" And then he was gone, his partner ahead of him carving a path through the crowd.

The trip to Captain Danilovitch's office was one they could have done without. The same secretary, a little uglier, sat in front of his office door. The scream of her electric typewriter had been replaced by the rapid-fire clicking of her fingertips against the keyboard of a desktop computer. As she picked up the telephone to tell

Danilovitch they were there, Lew looked over her shoulder at the four-color display of graph lines and tables of numbers crowding the bluish computer screen.

Lew couldn't stand it any longer, and asked her, "You really understand that?"

"Of course, Sergeant," she said, with a patient smile. "There's no magic to it. It's different, but it's not at all difficult. Would you like me to explain it for you?"

"Uh, no, ma'am, thanks, but we're in sort of a hurry here, we need to talk to the Captain. Maybe some other time, okay?" She tried, but couldn't subdue the knowing look in her eyes.

"Of course, Sergeant, some other time. He says to go right in."

As they entered, they saw Danilovitch putting down his pink bottle.

"I don't want to hear anything at all, except that you've got our killer. I just got off the phone with the Mayor, and he's pissed. He wants results, and he wants them as of yesterday. And now I do, too. Understood? Don't give me no shit, don't give me no jive, just give me results!"

Lew and Dan traded glances; this was a new Danilovitch, reacting less like the street cop he'd been, than a political cop about not to get a plum. They'd seen this sort of thing once before, when a political cop from back East had been appointed Chief. He'd only been there about two years, before moving on to another Chief's slot "up the career ladder" in California, but he had left behind a demoralized and politicized police department that took five years of hard effort by the present Chief to straighten out. They didn't like the thought that Danilovitch might be getting political; it was too much like fish flying.

At almost the same instant, Danilovitch's expression changed, and he said, "I'm sorry, Dan, you didn't have that coming. I'm taking my frustrations out on you. The mayor's jumping the command chain and eating my ass, the press is having a field day with this, and the PC just suggested that maybe I ought to retire if I'm not getting the job done. It's a lousy day."

"Yeah, well," Dan mused, "we know how that goes. So maybe we can brighten it up for you some. It's not all that big of a break yet, but we just got the ballistics on those hoods got blown away last

133

night. The same gun did them that did those other gang punks in the park. No connection we can see between the victims, but it looks like we got the same shooter. Not much, but something, huh?"

"Yeah," Danilovitch said, as he dropped his bulk into his chair "So what do you do with it?"

"Right now, maybe nothing, but like Lew said earlier, our boy's finally made his mistake. Look, Captain, all this time we've been chasing around after different weapons. Each time somebody got offed, if you only look at the shootings, we saw different guns. Now we got the same gun used again. What it suggests, see, it suggests our boy's running out of weaponry. That might also mean he's running out of ideas for different M.O.'s, which suggests maybe killings going down the same way."

* * * * * * * * *

When they returned, Lew picked up a large manila envelope laying on top of his files. He turned it over, read for a moment, then softly cursed. As he sighed heavily and dropped into his chair, Dan took notice of the change in him. "Hey, what's up, Bro?"

Lew dug into his pocket, pulled out some bills and crammed them into the envelope. He signed the back, then pitched it onto Dan's desk. "Camacho. Last night he ate his gun. This's for flowers."

Chapter 9

THE word out around the stylish Southhill Prado area was that, if you wanted some very good recreational substances (in this neighborhood nobody would call it dope, and heaven FORBID calling it "good shit"), the man to see was Artie. Nobody knew or bothered to ask for Artie's last name. Not at all important, as long as he was discrete, reliable, and honest. All of which Artie Fitzgerald was. He could get it all, from pot to heroin, with all stops in between. From medicinals to Columbian agricultural products. All good, all high quality, all clean. And all at a price. Artie, then, was definitely the man to see. And they did, coming from the plush condos, pricey boutiques and neighborhood offices of national stock brokerage houses that infested the Southhill Prado. Artie's conviction record was very short, which his arrest record wasn't. Nobody knew for sure whether Artie was just lucky, blessed or maybe had a little help that nobody knew about. All that was known was that the last two times Artie had been busted, neither trial resulted in a conviction. In one case the evidence had simply disappeared, and even Internal Affairs couldn't get to the bottom of it, and in the second, a directed verdict of acquittal had been dropped on him by a judge with no reputation for forgiveness whatsoever. And Artie wasn't much of a talker, so nobody was likely to know for sure. And in the Prado, prying would have been too gauche anyway.

This night was unusually warm, the sort of night that made you want to leave your windows open as you drove, the better to smell the lingering sweetness of the breezes. Also for practicality in Artie's case, so that he could hear a soft call from the sidewalk. Among the rounds that Artie made, his late evening run took place at about 10:45, right after the theaters let out and the restaurant crowd dwindled. As he paused at the stop sign at the corner of Seville and 90th, Artie checked the digital clock in his car radio, keeping himself on schedule. As with bus lines and air lines, dope dealers can't afford to be ahead of schedule. The customers can wait for you if you're a little late, but if you leave early they can't get to where it is they're going. And some of them really need to get there. Usually punctuality is a virtue — usually. This time around it didn't do Artie the first bit of good. In fact, you might say that punctuality did him in, since Lutie Mayfield and Homer Browning knew just where to be. It was just that easy, then, for Lutie to stand to Homer's left, so the 90th Street traffic couldn't see the gun, and for Homer to poke the silenced .32 Colt automatic through the open window. One shot behind Artie's left ear, the muffled report lost in the traffic sounds, and they stepped around the car, continuing west along 90th.

It wasn't until several minutes later that the light blue Cadillac pulled up behind Artie, and about a minute after that, before the well-dressed couple inside decided that, after all, the limits of courtesy had been reached. In fact, it took another minute or so of polite horn-honking, impolite horn-honking and then downright rude horn-honking, before the gentleman driving opened his car door and walked up to Artie's car to see what was holding things up. He saw what was holding things up.

In the time it took for him to rid himself of some used Chateaubriand, make his wife understand him and then get her to call in on the cellular phone, an elderly couple who wouldn't have drawn any notice anyway were on a Metro Transit bus headed north, toward an anonymous retirement home in the midtown area.

For Lew and Dan, it was just another exercise in futility. Nobody saw anything, nobody heard anything, and would the Police Department please remove all this, since it had an adverse impact upon the ambiance of the Prado? The private security force hired to patrol the Prado's real estate was most insistent that "all this" be removed, and the representative obliquely referred to his ability to exert pressure through the Mayor's office if this weren't cleaned up post-haste. To emphasize his seriousness, he smoothed his blazer with the gold thread embroidered badge in the left breast.

Not one bit of which impressed either Lew or Dan. In fact, if you're going to throw your clout around, it's best not to try it with street cops who should have been off duty several hours ago. They don't like it. They might not like you. They might tell you exactly where to stick it. And they did, they did just that.

"Listen up, white bread, no friggin' pansy rent-a-cop tells me what to do," Dan grumbled. "Now get your ass behind that yellow tape there, and if you so much as open your mouth, I'm gonna bust you for felony fairy."

Lew blandly looked up from where he was dusting the driver's side windowsill for prints. "Tch, tch, my goodness, Mister Perkins, how you do talk."

Dan extended his second finger from his fist, first vertically, then so it was pointing horizontally at Lew. "Yeah, and this's for the horse you rode in on, too," Dan grumbled. He bent down closer to look at where Lew was working. "You got something there?"

"I don't know, there's a partial here, smeared, pointing inward, may have something to it. If it'd been Fitzgerald's, it'd most likely be pointing outward, like when he'd grab the door to swing it closed." Lew pantomimed the action with his left hand. "So, maybe this'll come in handy. I wish to hell it could talk, is what I wish. God, when do we get a good break for our side?"

After spending 10 more minutes watching the crime scene crew dusting the rest of the surfaces without any luck, Lew straightened up, turned away and lit a cigarette.

Dan came around from where he'd been going through the other side of the car. "Well, it's not a total loss, look at all the shit I just harvested from under the seat and in the glove compartment. Sort of makes you wonder what else's stashed around inside these wheels, huh?" He turned to a uniformed sergeant and made arrangements. "This car stays under lock, two men on it at all times, overnight. You got that?"

"Yeah, okay, can do."

Lew appraised the contents of Dan's hands and said, "You know, if just a couple of grabs pulls that kind of stuff out from under the seats, you have to be impressed. Damn car makes the French Connection look like peanuts."

It was 1:30 by the time they were done. The private security cop had gotten the message an hour earlier, but they kept a slow pace just to rub it in. When there was finally nothing more they could do, they released the body to the M. E.'s crew, had the tow truck hooked up and moving away with a patrol unit directly behind, and then turned back to the dozen or so people left standing on the sidewalk. At Lew's inquiry as to which of them would like to tell if they saw or heard anything, they melted away into the night. Dan gave the Prado's security guard a bland look, then reached down and tore the yellow tape strung in his way. It fluttered to the sidewalk, laying across the guard's shoes. Dan made it a point to pause and look down at it, then turned and walked back to the car.

Lew had already started the engine, so Dan entered the right side. He slammed the door three times before it caught, then leaned his head back against the headrest.

"You're just not a good citizen, Dan, what am I gonna do about you?" Lew said.

"Huh?"

"I said you're not a good citizen. How the hell am I gonna explain to these high-falutin' types around here, why it is that my partner's a litter bug? You should be ashamed of yourself, throwing that barricade tape on the street and just leaving it there. Shame, shame, shame, Dan. You made that poor rent-a-cop have to clean up behind you. He's not gonna like that."

Dan opened one eye. "Fuck him. I don't even want to think about him. Coffee, pardner, lots of coffee," he mumbled as Lew pulled away. "Damn glad you're driving, 'cause I'm all used up. Even worse, there was a definitely attractive lady, of the feminine persuasion, bigger'n hell ain't gonna still be waiting for me at my apartment, no more, no more. The African Queen done pulled out without me."

Lew scanned the thin traffic, turned toward an all-night eatery he knew of in a less attractive part of town, then smiled. "Look at it this way, Dan, celibacy sharpens the mind. And yours needs all the sharpening it can get."

Chapter 16

LIEUTENANT Madigan had the shift. He didn't want the shift. He hated the shift. Which is probably why he got it. Madigan was night people from the word go. He could stay up until dawn, with what seemed to be increasing energy and mental alertness, and then crash at somewhere near 8 a.m., just like somebody had pulled his plug. Waking up at 6 a.m., as he had to for two weeks out of every six, was the most severe punishment anybody could inflict upon him. So it was a matter of self-preservation that he'd developed an understanding with the shift sergeants that they'd handle the routine stuff during the days and not bother him in his office except for unusual circumstances which would require the presence of a Lieutenant or higher. By Madigan's definition, non-routine occurrences began with World War III or events of higher magnitude. So he was understandably miffed that Sergeant Woleriez had disturbed his deep meditation at 9:05 a.m. to tell him about the little old lady the medics had gotten a call on.

They'd received a D.B. call from a foot patrolman in the little park downtown and gone over to pick her up. Since there were no signs of a struggle or other foul play, and the foot patrolman had found her while she was still warm, they'd just put her on the gurney, picked up her purse and knitting bag from the park bench and brought her to the morgue pending identification, notification of next-of-kin, possible autopsy if the M.E. thought it necessary, and all the other minor, routine details. It only left the realm of the routine when the M.E.'s crew, routinely going through and listing her belongings, added to "skein, wool, medium grey, unknown length," the notation, "Pistol, M1911A1, semiautomatic, caliber .45, serial number 2038332, w/seven (7) unexpended cartridges." Since little old ladies generally don't add heavy artillery to their knitting, Sergeant Wolericz disturbed Lieutenant Madigan.

Madigan read the initial report, then softly cursed the fates. Today he would not sleep. Today he would have to perform actual work in the daylight. Today he would probably come to the notice of somebody higher up. Today ... aw hell, today was ruined. He felt around under the desk with his feet, placed them back in his shoes, heaved himself up out of the chair and walked to the other end of the hallway where the squadroom was located. As he reached his objective, Lew looked up.

"What brings you out of your office in daylight, Lieutenant? Aren't you afraid the sun'll turn your body into dust? That's how Dracula bought it, you know. Terrible risk. Nobody carries silver bullets around any more, but daylight comes every 24 hours."

Madigan sighed. "Everybody likes a little ass, but nobody likes a smart ass, Perkins. I may be lazy, but I'm not stupid. We got a little old lady, died of what looks like natural causes in that downtown park just now. It wouldn't be anything, except they found a .45 in her stuff. Everybody knows you two hotshots're working this serial vigilante thing. I figure this's unusual enough, you might want to take a look at it. The hardware's on its way over. I'll leave a message with Property to let you know when it gets here. Otherwise, here's the initial report."

As Madigan turned away, Dan's eyes widened across the desk, his gaze fixed on the paper in Lew's hand. "Yeah, okay, thanks, Lieutenant, I appreciate it." Lew wasn't about to wait. He was on his feet with Dan barely a second behind, heading for Property.

* * * * * * * * *

"I dunno."

"You don't know? What the hell do you mean, you don't know? Fer Chrissakes, you got the gun, you got the brass, what the hell more do you want? C'mon, man," Lew said, "we need answers, not I dunno's."

Coppoldi looked up, scanned both Perkins, then turned to the right toward the projection screen. "Look," he said, as he turned on the projection switch to the comparison microscope. The wall illuminated with a split image, almost three feet across, of two halves of the back end of a cartridge, superimposed on each other. "This on the left is the known that we just fired off into the tank, this on the right is from the last shooting. Before we go any further, let's improve your education a little, so you'll understand what I'm up against, what I would have to be able to testify to." He pivoted off the tall stool and began to pace the floor between the wall and the table, clearly beginning a Wednesday lab in Criminalistics 402, which was what he taught at Central State.

"When a firearm, and here we're talking typical, modern cartridge weapons, is fired, several things happen. In order, they are: the firing pin falls on the primer; the primer ignites, thereby causing a small flash inside the cartridge case; that small flash ignites the propellant, which can be of any number of commercial mixes, which we'll ignore for now. Suffice to say that the propellant, as it burns, expands. That expansion of gases overcomes, first, the inertia of the seated bullet, second, the gripping pressure of the cannelure, or whatever method is used to mechanically crimp the bullet into the cartridge case, so it shouldn't fall out at some embarrassing moment. You still with me?"

"Okay. After overcoming those two factors, the bullet starts to move. If in a revolver, the bullet moves out of one of the chambers in the cylinder and, if in what we call an automatic, which is actually only semi-automatic, from the unrifled chamber portion of the barrel, into the rifled portion of the barrel. As it does with this weapon, the standard, old GI model .45. While this is going on, a couple of other things are happening: Newton's law about equal and opposite reactions is taking effect, and the cartridge case, or shell if you prefer, is being pushed backward, with a force equal to that of the bullet moving forward, and the pressure of the expanding gases inside the shell is minutely stretching the brass of the shell against the sides of the chamber. Happens all the time. Okay so far?"

They nodded. "Now let's go back to the bullet. That bullet starts to move forward until it encounters a series of grooves cut in a spiral manner down the length of the barrel. Depending on the make and model, there can be any number of grooves, the opposite of which, by the way, are called lands. Everybody got this so far? Good. Now the bullet is minutely larger than the space allowed by the lands. That causes the bullet's material, generally lead, to squeeze itself into the grooves. Without going into the physics and metallurgy of this thing, let's just say that because the width of the grooves and lands exceeds the depth, the material of the bullet doesn't just shear off. It moves a little, it bends a little, but it doesn't break. Instead, it flows into the grooves, it grabs on, and it makes the bullet follow the spiral of the grooves."

Dan opened his mouth to speak, but Coppoldi smiled and said, "You in the front row, siddown and shaddup. I talk, you listen, I teach, you try to learn," and kept on.

"So the bullet is now spinning as it moves forward, and now it gets to the end of the barrel. Out it pops, gyro-stabilized, on its way to wherever it was sent, and generally depending on the character of the shooter, it's either going into a paper target or into what we'll call the shootee. Ah, you may ask, is that all?"

Dan said, "Ah, is that all?" eliciting a smile from both Lew and Coppoldi.

"Glad you asked that question. No, that isn't all. For the sake of brevity, which I haven't been so far, let's just talk about our weapon here, this good old .45. You'll remember, in our earlier episode, that our brass shell was being worked on by several of Newton's laws. Well, one of those laws has now pressed the walls of the shell against the walls of the chamber."

"Look," Lew interjected, "I understand you're a genius in your field, and I already been through most of this at the academy. I don't want to know all about Newton's laws, I just want to know about this one gun. Can you tell me, or can't you, if this gun did the killings? That's all I need to know."

Coppoldi's voice turned a little sharper. "I know what you want to know. And after you're ready to understand it, you'll get your answer; but until then, sit down, shut up and try to learn something. Sometimes I honestly have to marvel at you guys. You're working on the premise that running around in circles and looking busy is the same as doing something constructive. Tell me, hot shot, where the hell are you going to be while I'm up on a witness stand trying to protect your shitty evidence from a high-bucks defense lawyer who plays juries like a harmonica? Out in the hall is where you'll be, munching hot dogs and cokes and telling lies, while I'm taking the heat for your bad case; that's where. So shut up already, and like I said, try to learn something."

Dan's voice broke in, in that conciliatory tone he'd developed, the one that could charm rabid wolves into fawning puppies, and all sorts of women into his bed. "He's right, Bro, the man's got a solid point. Let's hang loose here, maybe get something we can use, maybe get us a sense of direction. We can afford the time, if he'll afford us the know-how. Go on, Coppoldi, I apologize for both of us."

Somewhat mollified, Coppoldi returned to the projected image on the wall. "Where was I? Oh, yeah. So. That reaction of the bullet presses the soft brass against the breechblock, until the breechblock starts to move the whole slide assembly backward. While it's moving backward, a little finger, a hook-shaped thing, usually at about the three o'clock position, it's called the extractor, grabs the rim of the empty shell and starts to pull it out of the chamber. Since it's pressed in there by the expanded gases, it pulls kind of hard. And as it pulls out, it leaves a series of scratch marks from the imperfections in the chamber on the sides of the shell. Okay? You with me? So while the extractor's pulling the shell out, the initial pressure on the back of the cartridge has also embossed whatever toolmarks there were on the face of the breech-block, onto the back of the cartridge. Stay with me, now," he cautioned, "we're almost through. At the end of the stroke, there's a little stub, this one's called the ejector, that smacks the cartridge rim, generally around the six or the seven o'clock position, that flips it up and out of the mechanism. That gets rid of the expended shell just before the slide starts forward, picking up the next cartridge in the clip and sliding it forward and up into the chamber for the next shot. But just before the action closes, the extractor, which is kind of springy, slides its hook-shaped end over the rim of the cartridge. Then, last thing, the trigger's pulled, the hammer drops on the firing pin, the firing pin moves forward against the primer, and the next shot's on its way. You still with me on this?"

He took a breath, then continued: "I tell you all this so we've got some common ground to talk about. When we do a comparison study, now we got our choice, depending on what's available, to match up tool marks, imperfections, whatever. We got rifling marks on the bullet, we got chamber scratches on the shells, we got tool marks and scratches from the finishing process on the breech-block, the extractor, the ejector, we got marks on the firing pin that get transferred to the primer. We got all these things to go with, NORMALLY. And here's where it gets interesting, fellas. The rifling marks on the slugs from the earlier killings don't match this gun. The chamber marks on the brass don't match what I've got here. The breech-block markings don't match. In fact, I'd almost say they were changed with a file, or something similar, to judge by the way they're made. And the extractor and ejector marks, they also don't match. In fact, nothing matches, but one oddly shaped, almost spiral-type marking on the firing pin, which left this mark you see, right up here." He pointed to the screen outlining the primer and the firing pin mark. "But you'll also notice, these other scratches on the firing pin which overlay the one matching scratch." He took another deep breath, then climbed back onto his stool. "Gentlemen," he said. "You've got one, count 'em, one, matching characteristic to possibly, maybe, just-by-golly, by chance, tie this gun in to your vigilante killer. I can't take this into court. It just won't hold up in front of a jury, not even if the defense was a first-year law student, zonked out on whatever it is the kids smoke nowadays. It wouldn't work one bit."

"But privately, I'll tell you this: every gut feeling I have tells me you've got your vigilante killer, he's got spare parts for his gun, and to top it off, he's a pretty good gunsmith, as well."

Coppoldi rolled his head back and stared at the ceiling. "Except that he is a her, and according to the file you done brung me with that gun, she no longer is. She was." He snapped his gaze back down, pointed his finger at Lew and continued: "This little old lady, any chance she could be related to Wyatt Earp? Doc Holliday? Jesse James? Maybe, say, a distant relative to some other gunslinger? If not, Paisan, you're not a hell of a lot better off than you were before. Where you are ain't where you want to be."

"Oh, yeah, one more thing — when I got this piece, first thing I did was look in the barrel. There was powder residue. It's recently been fired. Now with what we know, what we figure about the guy, since he's got spare parts and all that, the fact that it wasn't clean tells me it was fired very recently. Otherwise, he'd have cleaned it. It's what, ten-fifteen now; my guess is that your guy might have iced somebody, then gave the old lady the gun. I think you got a shoot out there that hasn't been reported yet. God knows, in this city it wouldn't surprise me at all."

In the uncomfortable silence that followed, Dan studied his shoes for a moment "All right, so where are we?"

"Getting closer," Coppoldi said. "It's not over yet. What you've got so far is that the three hoods in the park were done with the same gun. No doubt about that one. The two hoods from last week, or was it two weeks ago, they were done by the same gun, as witness the matching brass, although with a different barrel in the gun. The slugs don't match. The brass does. Now, this here gun," he waved his hand at the piece on the table, "I think is the weapon used, although I can't prove it for lack of points of identification. It's like a partial fingerprint; not enough to convict, but just enough to aim you in the right direction. This stiff you got the gun off of, this, ah," he turned and read off the report form, "Emma Schechter, female, cauc, age 78, etcetera, either she did those guys, or she knows, pardon me, KNEW, who did, or she borrowed the piece from somebody who did, or something. I already called the M.E.'s boys, they're going to do a nitrate test on the old lady's hands, just in case it was her that fired the piece. If she didn't, then you guys find out that part, you've probably got yourselves a killer. You get a squeal on a recent shoot, I'd bet anything you've got the weapon in your hand."

Lew and Dan got up, picking up the lab report and the brass cartridges in their bags, as Coppoldi removed the test pieces from the comparison microscope and bagged them. "Here, take the gun, too, it goes with the paper. You know," he said, "you guys want to be careful. There wasn't print one on any of the brass, on any of the parts of the gun. Everything, every single surface, was wiped clean. No prints on the brass, the altered machined surfaces, the fact that he's got beaucoup spare parts," Coppoldi mused, "I feel like you're going after somebody's a real pro. Somebody dangerous as hell, very, very good, vicious as they come. Be damn careful, huh? This guy's a stone cold killer."

They had no sooner returned and sat down at their facing desks than Dan's phone rang. The conversation went like this:

"Detective Perkins. No, Dan ... Yeah ... Yeah ... Yeah ... Lemme guess ... Yeah, bigger'n shit ... Yeah, on our way."

Lew tensed and was on his feet as the phone hit the cradle. "Where was it?" he asked.

"Back of a building, 9th and Maryland." Dan reached for the car keys. "Called in by a garbage man, emptying dumpsters. With a big friggin' exit wound. Like from a .45."

Dan affected a nonchalant walk down the steps to the car, with his hands in his pockets, purposely humming a tune from "Snow White": "Hi ho, Hi ho, it's off to work we go..."

As Lew got in the car, he slammed the door twice to make it catch, and said, "Let me guess, Dan, the victim's a bad guy, isn't he? Goddamn door, let's get this fixed. It's dangerous."

Dan was smiling as he absently waved his hand toward Lew. "Yeah, we got to do that." Then he cupped his hand behind his right ear. "Hey, Bro, you hear singing, my man? Sounds like a fat lady."

* * * * * * * * *

"Somebody stalked him. That's the only explanation I can give you on this one, Lew." Detective 2nd Edith McCahan twisted her head both ways, looking up and down the alley. "Look. This alley's just crooked enough, there's no seeing from one end to the other. Nothing in around here but these two dumpsters, this one, and that one behind the Italian restaurant. This door here, this leads down to the basement of the office building. No, we already looked. Nothing down there out of the ordinary. So what was a mob heavyweight doing here? Was he meeting somebody, doing some business down there, was it a quiet way to get into the building to meet somebody in one of the offices upstairs? God, I don't know, and we may never know. But what we do have, is we've got Angelo Tedesco, with a bullet hole in his back, right here at the doorway. We'll need an opinion from the M.E. on when he died. For right now, all I can do for you is the usual crime scene work, maybe get lucky when we sweep the alley for evidence. You got any ideas, I'll be happy to assist if you want to take command on this one."

Dan was lost in thought as Lew demurred. "No, Edie, you've got it. It's probably going to fall in with our vigilante thing, but for now I'd just as soon we didn't jump into it."

At length Dan stopped looking up and down the alley and spoke: "Either stalked or ambushed. Look, this was a hard guy; he'd have been streetwise enough to recognize that somebody was walking behind him. Let's guess, he was packing heat, right?"

McCahan smiled. "Foxy old devil, you peeked, didn't you? He's still got it on him."

"No," Dan continued, "it just figures. So, anyway, if he didn't reach, and he didn't try to avoid or evade, then the most likely answer that comes to mind is that he didn't recognize a threat. He didn't see the ghost of J.Edgar Hoover behind him, or any of Al Capone's heirs either."

Lew broke in with, "Yeah, and he didn't see Mary Poppins either, so where are you going with this?"

Dan turned to him, absently tapping a fingertip against his nose. "No, Lew, where I'm going is, maybe he DID see Mary Poppins. See, in the absence of any reason for him to be alarmed or suspicious, he would have had to have been shot by somebody he knows, somebody he wouldn't think anything about turning his back on, or somebody he wouldn't EXPECT to be dangerous."

Lew jumped onto Dan's train of thought. "Bigger 'n hell, Dan. Now I see where you're going with this. Would anybody at all, ever, get worried about, say, some little old bag lady, going through garbage cans here, maybe looking into a dumpster, maybe just plunked down, say, sitting against a wall? Hell, no, he'd take one look and then pass on."

For the space of a heartbeat, they looked at each other, then said simultaneously, "Emma Schechter."

Lew quickly filled McCahan in on who Emma Schechter was and her unique choice in knitting accessories. As they talked, they unconsciously moved over to the most likely point where a gunman would have been standing to have nailed Angelo Tedesco while he was facing the door. Then all three did the same thing. They aimed their empty hands, forefingers outstretched, at the ghost of a standing Angelo. Each dropped a thumb, mimicking the drop of a gun's hammer, and each turned to the right, where a .45 would have ejected an empty shell. After about two minutes' looking, McCahan grunted and stood up. "Here we go, gents, here it is. It was in a crack in the concrete under the dumpster."

Dan reached out and took it from her outstretched hand. "You done good, Edie, we owe you for this one. Look, you do the rest of the work-up here, okay? We need to get this brass over to the lab. What'll you bet this's Emma's brass?"

"No bet, Dan," Lew smiled, "Nary a one."

As they left the alley, Dan looked back. McCahan was talking to two uniforms, gesturing at the body and clearly running the show. "What'll you bet she finds the slug?"

"No bet there either. She'll find it just to tie up the loose ends, but we won't need it. This, my man, is the key. I can feel it in my gut. From here on in, we can't lose. You listen close, you can hear the fat lady singing louder now."

By the next three hours, Lew and Dan knew all there was to know about Emma Schechter, which was that she was not a licensed driver, had no credit cards, had no arrest record, was on Social Security, her bank book showed $841.63 at First Merchant's, and that she lived (had lived) at a small nursing and retirement home near mid-town that had been licensed 30 years ago and annually inspected with nothing notable to report. Oh, yeah, also that the gun in her knitting bag had killed Angelo Tedesco. In short, Emma Schechter was a nice little old lady largely retired from the world, packing and using heat. And she didn't even wear tennis shoes, as Lew wryly observed.

Chapter 17

As they walked up the front steps of the Forest Fen, Lew's hand slipped into his suit coat and unsnapped the strap holding his weapon in its holster. He felt foolish and hoped his partner wouldn't notice. While he was feeling foolish, he missed Dan's hand coming out from under his topcoat.

Once through the double doors they found themselves in a small lobby, filled with overstuffed chairs and furniture left over from a period long ago. It was as if the inhabitants and their furnishings were all of the same vintage, until they saw a modern-looking counter at the side and a nurse's cap bobbing up and down behind it. They walked there and saw who was under the cap. The nurse there wore a stiff white dress with an antique-looking nursing school pin, blue hair and wire-framed bifocals. Dan remembered reading somewhere that the shapes of nurses' caps were distinctive, and that they told what nursing school they'd gone to. He made a mental note to look that one up some day. The nurse looked only a few days younger than their quick average-age estimate of the residents they saw around them.

She looked up and said, "May I help you, young man?"

The tone of her voice transported Lew back to Our Lady Queen of Peace. In that instant he regressed from Detective 1st to 5th grader, and the short, bird-like nurse turned into Sister Mary Bridget. "Uh, yes, ma'am, uh, we're police officers, uh, we'd like to, uh, speak to the, uh, director, here, uh, on a police matter."

She looked up at him sharply. "Is there something wrong?"

"Well, yes, ma'am, uh, we have to notify your, uh, is it director? of the death of one of your, uh, residents. If you'll announce us, please, ma'am?" Now that he was onto more familiar ground, Lew began to feel like an adult again.

The nurse looked flustered, and said, "Oh, dear, that's awful," and looked down at a Rolodex file in front of her. Dan noticed that she appeared to be reading intently. Almost as if she'd been bounced out of the chair, the nurse was up on her feet, moving around the counter. Dan also noticed that, before she moved away from the desk, she gave the Rolodex a twirl.

The room they entered matched what they had expected from seeing the lobby and the residents. Old wall pictures, old furniture, drapes pulled halfway across tall windows, a rug showing thread-bare areas, all served to set the mood of the room. The phrase that ran through Lew's mind was "shabby-genteel," although he admitted to himself that he didn't really know what that meant. At the far end of the room sat a slight, mostly bald-headed elderly man who fit the room. Quiet, somber-looking, a leftover from another time. As they drew closer, Lew could see the man was wearing a three-piece suit that looked about two sizes too big. An old-fashioned collar clip glinted under the knot of the narrow, darkly striped tie.

He looked up as they approached. "Mr. Handelman," the nurse intoned, "these men are from the Police. They're here about Mrs. Schechter."

Dan and Lew exchanged quick glances, picking up on the fact that they hadn't told the nurse who had died. Lew held out his badge folder. "My name is Lew Perkins, sir, and this is my partner, Detective Dan Perkins. Not related. We came to report the death of one of your residents. Do you know a Mrs. Emma Schechter?"

Handelman's face showed no emotion. "Yes," he said, "she was one of ours. I'm sorry to hear that she is dead. How did it happen?"

Lew caught a hint of an accent, classified it as European, but couldn't come up with a country.

Dan answered, "She passed away peacefully, down in Harvey Park, at about nine o'clock this morning. The Medical Examiner is holding the body. I assume you'll want to make arrangements?"

"Yes, of course," Handelman answered. "Miss Bradford, will you notify the others that we have lost Mrs. Schechter? I should tell you, gentlemen, that this is a rather commonplace thing for us. We, all of us, have come here to finish out our days, and the thought of dying holds no terrors for us. We are all of us ready to go, at the time God chooses, and how He chooses. You are yet young, so this is perhaps difficult for you to accept. We who are old have already learned to accept much. This is just one more thing." Handelman rose and held out his hand. "Thank you for coming, gentlemen. I appreciate your thoughtfulness."

Lew's hands stayed at his sides. "There's another matter we'd like to discuss with you, Mr. Handelman. When Mrs. Schechter died, she was pretty far away from here. Did she have some errand or something, that she was going downtown for? I mean, why would she be there?" Dan caught the quick reaction in Handelman's eyes as Lew spoke. The twitch would have gone unnoticed if Dan hadn't been looking for it. Cool dude, he thought, this cat's not coming. But he sure as hell knows something.

"She could have been there for any reason at all, Mr. Perkins, any reason at all. We are, as I am sure you have noticed, all adults here. We are free to come and go as we please, with no restrictions. Those of us who need no assistance lead quite active lives, I assure you. She could have wanted to go shopping, to a movie downtown, maybe to the library, who knows? We are too old here for limits other than those we impose upon ourselves. So I'm afraid I can't help you. Is there anything else? I shall have to start making arrangements, you see."

Lew's voice dropped and went flat, carrying with it the tone he often used in interrogations. "No more games, Handelman. We got the gun. Why the gun? Why did she have it? And don't tell me for self-protection. Little old ladies don't carry cannons in their purses."

Handelman sat down again, sighed and spread his hands at shoulder level in an expressive gesture. "I was hoping you didn't have it. I'm sorry. But then, I suppose, since it's over, there is no longer any harm. The answer is very simple, gentlemen. Emma Schechter had the gun because she was going to kill someone." He allowed himself a gentle smile. That is what you wanted to know, is it not?"

Dan cut in: "Correction. She DID kill someone."

"In that case then, I should guess, Mr. Perkins, that after she did, she became excited, she sat down — in the park, you say? And her poor dear heart, it would have just given out." With an effort, Handelman eased himself to his feet, walked around from behind the desk and sat down in a high-backed wing chair.

"You knew? You knew this was going on? What the hell is all this?" Dan's voice was incredulous. "What gives here?"

Handelman steepled his fingers over his chest and looked up at them. "It is very simple, gentlemen. You are looking for a killer. Emma was such a one as you seek. So were others."

"Come, gentlemen, please," he said, "sit down with me. You can be relaxed; I'm certainly no threat to you. I wouldn't harm you anyway, even if I could. That is not what we are about, you see."

They gingerly sat on the Victorian sofa, across from a wall almost solid with bookshelves. Dan kept most of his weight on his feet, just in case.

"Mr. Handelman," Lew began, "let me advise you of your rights. You have the right to remain silent. If you give up the right to remain silent, you have the right to have an attorney present ..."

Handelman chuckled. "Yes, yes, I know, I know my rights, I know how it goes. What I don't pick up from reading, I get from television. I assure you, my young friend, I know my rights."

Lew pressed on, overriding Handelman's protestations, until he'd finished: "With the understanding of these rights as I've explained them to you, do you wish to waive your rights?"

Handelman pressed his fingertips together under his chin. "Of course, if you will slow down enough to let me. I've just told you we have been killing those criminals out there, but you won't let me get a word in edgewise. Is it written somewhere that we can't discuss this in a rational manner? Where is it written? If not, let us talk.

"To begin with, you have told me that Emma Schechter is dead, you have also told me that you have the gun she was carrying, no? And if you have the gun, you will probably have tested it, and you'll know ... you'll know what? It's not traceable, the bullets from the gun will not match any of the others, you'll have no evidence, you will be at a dead end. But, my young friends, I will tell you this:" His voice turned up, into a singsong pattern, "I will tell you that you are right, I will tell you that we have been cleaning up the streets, I will even tell you who did what killings, you'll pardon, I

152

would rather call them executions. I will tell you whatever you want to know," he chuckled again. "I will tell you everything but where the physical evidence is that you need to prove your case. If necessary, that information goes to the grave with us. And from what you'll look and you'll see, for some of us that could be next week, tomorrow, maybe even tonight, maybe even, God wants it so, right before your eyes."

As Handelman spoke, the door opened and he shifted his attention to the far end of the room. "Ah, ladies and gentlemen, come in, please. These gentlemen are police detectives. They have come about Emma Schechter, God rest her soul, and also about the removal of some garbage from our streets. I hope you won't mind, but I have just made a full confession on your behalf, also on my own, to all the executions we have performed." He turned his attention back to Lew and Dan, who were still trying to absorb everything they'd heard so far. "So, gentlemen, here we are." He waved one thin arm around the room. "We are your killers, all of us, each of us, singly and in concert."

Lew held out both hands, palms out. "Whoa, hold it, time out. Are you trying to tell me that these old," he paused to change his choice of words, "folks have been running around the city, knocking off all the bad guys? Hey, go a little farther and tell me about the tooth fairy. Pardon the expression, sir, but this's pure bullshit. I don't believe it."

"Oh, yeah? Well, try this on, son. Do I look at all familiar?" A voice by the door caught his attention. He looked, but couldn't quite put his finger on it. A small bell rang, but not enough to give him any specifics. "Uh, sort of, but I can't place you."

"Well, how'd it be if I told you I turned in the call on those three hoods got wiped away in the park last summer? How'd it be if I told you that the punk got took out in the auto junkyard got it right next to a blue Pinto? Huh? Think that'd help you some? Name's McMorriss, son, Charlie McMorriss," he cackled.

Howard Kirk leaned forward from the chair he occupied and caught Dan's attention. "All those hits with .45's , you think they were all unconnected? Hell, son, that's my gun, even though you can't prove it. I brought it home after the war, kept it with me ever since. I had enough spare parts for it that I could change the bar-

153

rels whenever necessary, swap extractors, do whatever I needed, to keep you boys off balance." He leaned back, looking pleased. "Thought it was a whole bunch of guns, didn't you?"

Dan's mind jumped from A to E again. "You don't have any spare firing pins, do you?"

"Nope. They break awful easy. Best I could do was, I'd go over the tip with coarse sandpaper, just enough to change the markings. You're bright, young fella, real bright. Shows there's some hope for the younger generation yet," he laughed, dissolving into a coughing fit. "But you'll never be able to prove anything," he wheezed.

"Okay, how about the others?" Lew started to nudge, looking for as much information as he could get. "You still going to con me into believing you did all those killings? Hell, some of those were by stabbings, some were with automatic weapons. I'm not about to believe you're that tough, or that you've got access to that sort of armament. No way."

Kirk shook his head as he stifled the last of his coughing. "Son, in here we've had residents who were infantrymen in two wars, paratroopers, a couple of Marines, we even had us an old OSS agent and, oh yeah, even one leftover from the Imperial Japanese Army, immigrated here right about 30 years ago and started his own landscaping business. Son, we've had access to skills here that'd make your young blood run cold. What I'm trying to tell you is that you don't have to be big and tough, just skilled. And willing."

Before anyone else could speak, Handelman broke in : "You may believe what you wish, Mr. Perkins, we will give you any answers, any confessions you want. We will not, however, supply you with any evidence, nor will we expose to you our sources of supply. That information goes to the grave with each of us. As I mentioned a few minutes ago," he noted dryly, "that could be in a very few hours even."

The directness with which they spoke began to sink in to Lew. He was beginning to believe. These old people, they really HAD been killing off the bad guys. Nobody'd make up something like that, and sure as hell, nobody's ever gonna believe it either, his mind told him.

"The fact that you claim to have killed them doesn't stand alone. There're a lot of other questions to be answered first. For instance, how did you spot them, how did you know who they were, all that? How do you answer that part of the puzzle?"

A woman who looked vaguely familiar to Dan but hadn't really made an impression on his consciousness spoke up. "That was the simplest of all, Sport, it really was. If you want books, you go to the library. If you want criminals escaping from justice, you go to the courthouse. There were three of us, I was one of them. The other two are here in this room, but they'll have to identify themselves for you. I won't. Anyway," she continued, "we hung around the court-house, sitting in on trials. Whenever somebody beat the rap through some kind of trickery, we were right there to know who he was. And one of us, which I suppose might give something away, but who cares, retired from there, so we knew how to get all the infor-mation we needed."

Another woman spoke up: "In case you — no, not you, the other one there, I didn't catch your name, in case you might remember, you even sat down next to me. It's no secret, my name's Bea Haggerty. I started working there before you were born, most likely. That was the Mellon trial. Remember me now?"

Dan remembered. The courtroom, the case, the pandemonium when Mellon's accuser changed his testimony, all came back. And then in one of those mental flashes he could never explain, Dan also remembered what he'd heard her say after the judge said he expected to see Mellon again: "No, you won't, Freddie, no, you won't."

"Then you're going to hit Mellon?"

"That sure seems like a good idea, doesn't it?" she asked.

Dan shook his head emphatically, from side to side. "No. No, uh uh, no way. That's against the law. You can't do that."

One of the others spoke up. "Who's gonna stop us? You? How're you gonna do that? You can't tail all of us, and you can't protect him forever. Some one of these days, that little pup's gonna get his, and there's no way you can stop it." The speaker, an old man, held up an imaginary rifle, sighting with one eye closed. "Pow." He smiled, then, with an easy friendliness, "Nail him in a public place, the real crime'd be littering, not murder. Hell, he's garbage, and you know it. And there's nothing for us to lose either. We've already lived."

Lew stood up. He scanned carefully, looking into each elderly face, looking for something, he didn't know what. Then it struck him, he was looking for that sullenness, that defiance he'd always seen in any criminal he'd ever met. Some defiant spark, some attitude, some drive for conflict. What he saw was calm, pleasant, warm. Jesus, he thought, they look like Wednesday prayer meeting, not Murder Incorporated. He walked to the window and looked out at the failing light. Just like they are, he mused. They're fading about like the sunlight. What is it they call it, the twilight years? Nice old ladies, nice old gaffers, ought to be playing checkers, maybe knitting, doing whatever, and they're out there on the street instead, like some geriatric James Gang.

The irreverent portion of his mind, that part he'd long since given up trying to discipline, jumped into his thoughts with a picture of Red Riding Hood's granny, pulling a .45 out of her knitting bag and the wolf saying, "Oh, Granny, what a big cannon you have," and Granny saying, "The better to blow your ass away, Wolfie."

He smiled grimly to himself, then sighed and turned back to face them. "You've told us that you did it, and you've told us how, but you haven't told us yet, why. Why is it that folks who should be rocking, maybe knitting, resting or whatever, are going around committing systematic murder? I got to say this again: murder. Because that's what you've been doing. Not executions; that's something done by the state. Not cleaning up the streets; that's when you pick up candy wrappers and newspapers and such. Killing people without proper legal justification is murder. For God's sake, why? Huh? Just why did you do it?"

Handelman smiled that gentle smile again. "For God's sake. What a perfect choice of words, my young friend. For who else should we be doing this? For us? Nonsense. We can't live long enough to enjoy it. Let me put it this way: We were placed on earth by God. He gave us certain basic instructions in the beginning. Be fruitful and multiply, have dominion over the beings of the earth. In short, populate this earth and create a livable system. Did we do well? We did not. He saw what we had done, and He brought the flood, to start over. This we did, although only somewhat better. He watched my people as we ran ourselves under the heel of a conqueror and became a nation of slaves. He brought us out of slavery, gave us another chance. He taught us to be strong, and for a while we were. Do you remember Joshua? God's hornet, they called him. David,

Solomon, they did well. Mankind did well for a little while, but not very well. Plagues, famines, wars, ignorance, all combined to bring mankind to more ruin. Constantly we see such happening in this world. We have even become used to it.

"But there is a way to cleanse, to purify this world of at least some of these vermin. In a small way, we do our part. There is, in another language you wouldn't know, the word 'mitzvah.' It means a good thing to do, a thing of merit. So, my young friends, this is our mitzvah. We cleanse in the name of God, for His sake, with fire and sword ..."

Dan could feel the tension rising in the room. As he looked around, he saw how Handelman was affecting the rest of these old people. They were stirring and restless, drawing on reserves of energy that he didn't believe could have been present in people who'd looked so tired and feeble when he and Lew came into the building. Subconsciously he wondered which state was real. He snapped back in time to hear Handelman speaking again: "Let me tell you how all this came about. Obviously, we did not do all this for entertainment."

"You will recall, or perhaps not, since policemen in this city are kept so very busy, about two years ago a rash of strong-arm robberies took place. For the first few days of each month, armed and even un-armed thugs preyed upon the elderly and the incapacitated, taking away from them their Social Security, their monthly pension checks.

"In one case a member of our small community here was se-verely beaten by those scum. And do you want to know for what? I tell you: for thirty-eight dollars and fourteen cents. That was what she had left of her small pension check. For thirty-eight dollars and that pitiful amount of change, that woman, did I mention to you that she was over 80? That woman was knocked to the ground, her hip was broken, her eyes were blackened, they even took her wed-ding band, so old and worn it could have brought nothing in a pawn shop. But they took from her everything she had. This is tragic, yes? This is enough to make you angry, yes? No, gentlemen, not quite. You do not achieve anger yet. I will not let you. You achieve anger when I tell you that this all took place two blocks from here, on Main Street, at three o'clock in the afternoon, in full view of people on the street.

As Handelman spoke, Lew watched the change take place in his face. It was subtle at first, but Handelman's color changed from pale and gray to ruddy pink. He sat up straighter in the chair, breathing deeply, and his rheumy, faded eyes began to take on a life of their own. They became clearer looking, moving sharply, focusing directly on Lew. It crossed Lew's mind that anger was the source of Handelman's vigor.

"A little anger, is there? Ah, not yet, gentlemen, not yet. For the full effect of the anger, let me continue. Let me finish by telling you that not one person came to her aid, either during or after this mugging, and she had to drag herself into the grocery store there and beg for help. Now, gentlemen, I give you a gift, as it were, your anger. But, of course, only after I tell you that she never recovered. She died four months later.

"From this, we became more conscious of the increasing savagery growing in this city, this country, this world. Not that we were totally unaware of it prior to then," he smiled, "we are not that naive here. But it became clear to us that something must be done. Somehow, we must make the savagery stop. Are we not civilized in this world? Are we to abdicate, to give over the entire world to these scum, these savages? If so, what is to become of those who are either unable, or unwilling, to fight back? Do they just die? Does the world revert to some primeval state where only the strongest survive? Does brutishness overcome truth, beauty and the constructiveness of the human spirit?

"No, gentlemen, it cannot be permitted to be so: that is not civilization. And so, as a group, we remembered previous savagery, the why of it, how it was permitted to flourish, and how in some cases it was stopped."

He smiled sadly and pushed up his sleeve, showing a faded number tattooed on his forearm. "We have a strong collective memory of inhumanity, each of us, in one form or another. There are several of these tattoos in this house," he said, as he pushed his sleeve down. "I only tell you this because some of them can no longer speak for themselves. It could have been stopped in the early days. We had the numbers, we had the strength, what we did not have was the will. We were too busy with something else. Other things came first. And suddenly there was no one left to stop that madman, to end that nightmare in Germany, and then we were all behind barbed wire.

"People who didn't have other things to do, they had to come from across the ocean to stop him and rescue what was left of us. Even then, there were some in Europe who could have helped, but didn't. They turned their heads, they looked the other way. It wasn't convenient. It wasn't appropriate. It would violate their neutrality. It was a risk to their moral authority. Dear God, what good is moral authority if it isn't used? No matter; whether they could not or would not help, in either case the result was the same. They did not help. But we survived, some of us. Over six million did not, but some of us did." He leaned back and sighed. "Enough, enough, I am turning into a garrulous old Jew, dwelling upon the past."

Then he popped forward, transfixing Lew with his intense stare. "You want more than one instance? I give you Russia, I give you Stalin. I give you Mussolini. After World War Two, there was more. There was Mao Tse Tung, who knows how many he killed? The Chinese themselves, even they don't know. There was, what's his name? Invaded South Korea, started a war. You are both of an age to have been in southeast Asia; do you ever think of the North Vietnamese? Do you ever think about Cambodia?"

Another voice spoke up. "It isn't just political, either. Right here in this country of ours, we've never been invaded, but we're held hostage just the same. We've got organized crime, we've got drug dealers, we've got armed robbers, people'd bust you over the head for a dollar, they're just as bad."

Handelman picked up the thread again. "Here there are sadists, they beat people, they kill for the amusement of it, they beat and kill for money to pump poison into their veins, here there are even, God forbid, people, they … they beat and kill their own children, out of rage at who-knows-what, but they take it out on babies. Here there are even yet people who for sexual thrills, they use children. CHILDREN, for the love of God, how can they?" In the general murmur of agreement from the others, his voice dropped back down to a conversational tone.

"And do you know what they all have in common? They are garbage. They were garbage coming up, they are garbage now, and when they die they will just be so much garbage again. And they are what they are because we permit them to be so. Do you understand that?

Do you, as a policeman, understand, that if we don't permit that, then the garbage becomes less and less?" His eyes flicked across the room. Sad, pleading eyes.

A woman's soft voice took up, coming from Dan's left. "We helped make the world what it is, and we have to take that part of the responsibility for it. But we don't have to let it stay this way for our children. We can clean it up. Maybe just a little at a time, but it's something we can do. We can fight back."

"So you see," Handelman continued, "as we are the creations of God, as He created both good and evil, He also created the means to correct the problem. If He allows evil to exist, it is because He wants it so. If all this were not allowed by Him, we would not be here. Perhaps He would not have even allowed any of us to be born, to come together here. But we are, and we are here, and we are doing what must be done. And if He permits it, this purging of evil, who are you to stop it?"

"Let me assure you though," he continued, "we do not do this indiscriminately. In each case, we have looked carefully at the situation. We have observed those who twisted the law for their own ends, those who have escaped justice. Only those have we gone after, and in each case we have been more merciful to them than they have been to their own victims. We do not torture, we do not inflict unnecessary suffering. We merely apply the death penalty to those who need it."

"And in the case of some of those who were not professional criminals, they were in the commission of a crime when they were, ah, removed. Had they not chosen to commit their crimes, they could have walked away unhurt. We merely proved to them that it was dangerous to be criminals. No one who did not need killing was killed. And because of us, it is a little safer to walk the streets of this city.

"You are Christians, are you not? In your New Testament, you have Jesus saying that the meek shall inherit the earth. Later, you have Him advising to turn the other cheek. No, my son, I much prefer the Old Testament, wherein we are advised, 'an eye for an eye, a tooth for a tooth.' We have already been meek. Where has it gotten us? Moreover, where has it gotten you, except for harder work to control the scum of this world? We have been meek, my boy, and

160

it does not work. Now, we fight back. We are meek no more. We will strike to defend ourselves, both as individuals and as members of society." His voice was rising, and Lew found it almost compelling. "We will offer ourselves up as victims no more. WE WILL DEFEND OURSELVES. WE WILL STRIKE BACK!"

The look in Handelman's eyes, as well as the tone of his voice, were no act, Dan thought. "This old coot's absolutely sincere. He really believes in what he's doing, and these others are just following him along. Jeez, this's the flip side of Hitler. How the hell does it happen this nice old guy goes sour, turns bad?

Lew spoke up: "Look, I hear what you say, but this's all wrong. It's wrong from every viewpoint you choose. It's legally wrong, it's morally wrong. Who appointed you to be judge, jury and executioners?"

"Who appointed us to be the makers of this world?" Handelman asked. "We are, because we exist. Do you, can you, understand the principle? The world either sinks into darkness or it achieves, based upon what the people on it do. If they choose evil, such is what they will make, no matter what. If they choose good, then the means by which they achieve it, although suspect, will work. If the intent is good, the act itself is good." He shrugged. "I don't take credit for that, it was uttered long before you were born, by a European philosopher."

"How do I convince you? Consider: you are armed, and you walk into a situation that requires you kill someone. If he was evil, then your act has been good. Even though we are taught that it is inherently wrong to kill. You have cleaned up a little of the garbage. And if you have done so in self-defense or in defense of another's life, then your act is not punishable. This is only what we have done. Each removal of garbage from the city's streets has been in defense of ourselves, as members of society. We have protected ourselves from the next life-shattering crime those scum would have committed. And the muggers? They would have killed any of us. We are, for the most part, frail and weak. We could not have defended from them."

Dan answered, "But you didn't have to be there. You deliberately walked into areas where you were going to get mugged. You brought it on yourselves."

Handelman smiled sadly at him again. "Did you hear, young man, what you just said? You suggested that we were somehow at fault for being there. Is it written somewhere that we must give up the right to freely walk wherever we choose, just so that we shouldn't provoke some criminal?"

"Yeah," came another voice, "that's just like saying a rape victim had it coming somehow, because she was in the wrong place at the wrong time, or she didn't have enough bars on her windows. Or that a robbery victim shouldn't have been carrying all that money on him in the first place. You gonna tell me I gotta give up my life, go hide someplace, just to be safe? Uh, uh, sonny boy, my people came here in wagons, they fought off Indians, droughts, floods, jayhawkers, anything they had to for what they wanted to keep. I may be too old to arm-rassle these hoods, but I'll damn sure fight back any way I can."

"Yeah, that's right," came another voice, followed by a general murmur of assent. "Besides, we got nothing to lose. It's just like the rest of life. It's a gamble. If we win, we cleaned up the streets some. If we lose, well, we died a little earlier, is all."

Lew shouted them down. "Hold it, hold it. You people are still missing the whole boat. You've been breaking the law. It's our job to uphold the law. We can't let you just walk away smiling and go on doing what you're doing. Nobody deserves to lose their life without a trial."

A chain-smoking old woman in a faded, flowery housedress waved her hand at him, catching his attention. Through the cigarette smoke he took in her deep-dyed black hair, somehow incongruous against the elderly plainness of her face. The sheer power in her posture, so erect and sure, impressed him. "You think an old lady, beaten to death for a few bucks, got a trial? You think some child, born blind or retarded or incomplete, maybe can't ever grow up, because its mother filled its veins with drugs before it was born, got a trial? You think some kid run over by a junkie in his car got a trial? Who speaks for them? Who is there to defend them, to see they get some justice? You can't do it, son, there aren't enough cops in the whole world to do it.

"But we can. And I'll tell you something else, Son, something that'll make you feel warm all over. We ain't all there is. You start

162

checking with other cities, you might find there's gonna be a run on hoods and scum in other places, too. We got a lot of time on our hands, time to write letters to people we know, people just like us, who've had enough, got nothing to lose, maybe want to leave a little better world behind when they go. See, you might be able to stop a few of us, but how're you gonna stop a whole generation? Huh?" The old woman folded her arms against her bosom and leaned back against the wall. "Think about that," she said.

Handelman pointed to Dan. "And you, my son, are you untouched by all this? No. For you, there were those in the South, some in the North, they wore sheets to hide their faces while they beat and killed your people. Still they do these things wherever they are stronger than those opposing them, or where there is a lack of sentiment to make them stop.

"And there, my young friends, you have the key words: to make them stop. To make them do those things no more. We have laws against those things, yes, but how successful are they? We see every day that those who can afford the best lawyers, no matter where their money came from, they can go into courtrooms and come out free men. They can pay the price for their freedom, then go out and continue what they do. And you know that they can. They can even become rich. Those who deal in drugs, they make 50, a hundred times what a policeman makes. So. They do what they do, my son, and we do what we do."

"You can't," Dan broke in. "You can't because then you reduce society to the level of violence for violence, with no rule of law to live by. That's just the law of the jungle, man. If you do that, you're no better than they are. See, when you do it, you do it on your own. When we do it, we speak for society, for all the people, and we go by the rules of a civilized society. Maybe it doesn't always work out the way we want it to, but it's the way things have to be. Stop," he whispered, "you got to stop."

"And if we do stop, what then?" Handelman asked. "Do we let the garbage take over the streets again? Do we run and hide from everyone? What would you have us do?"

Dan shook his head. "I don't know. Some things, nobody's got the answers. All I know is, you've got to stop taking the law in your own hands, and you can't let this ... this thing spread to anyplace else."

Handelman leaned forward, his glasses reflecting thin slices of light from the desk lamp. "And you, my young friends, what will you do with us? Are we to be arrested and tried, almost certainly put into prison? Perhaps executed? How will you deal with us?"

"I don't know," Lew said.

"I suggest, therefore," Handelman said, "that there is truly little you can do. You have poor Emma Schechter, and you have the pistol she used, but nothing else. We can, if necessary, all confess to each killing, and thereby diffuse and devalue any focal point of your investigation. I propose, then, a compromise. I propose that we shall kill no more, while we allow you time to ... to what? To control these scum? To perhaps effect a turnaround in society? Perhaps. Yes, I think, why not? Subject, of course to the assent of our members here.

"But I warn you, my son, we are a growing segment of society. As our numbers increase, so does the likelihood of a collective anger. And since we come closer each day to our last day, we have less and less to lose. Move quickly, my son. Either start the cleansing of our society, or we will do it for you."

* * * * * * * * *

As they walked down the front steps into the early December darkness, Lew mulled over what he had heard inside. "Jesus, what do we do now? How the hell do we handle this? We can't round up the whole damn nursing home. And we can't just let them get away with this. God, talk about a rock and a hard place, this is it." They climbed into the car, Dan slamming the right door three times to get it to shut.

"Freakin' door."

"C'mon, Dan, I need some input. What the hell do we do with this?"

Dan's reactions were slow in coming. "Not sure, Bro, seems to me we've got us a real poser here. I'd sure like to clear these cases. No problem there. But with what? We take those old folks in, hell, half of 'em'd never make the first 30 days. And even then, what do we book 'em on? Can you just see us bringing in a whole raft of creaky bones, half of them on canes or crutches, in cuffs? Hell, it'd be just like shooting Santa Claus to put that bunch on trial. And even then, murder one? Bullshit, my man. How'd you ever get a D.A. to go on that?

"You know," Dan continued, "that old Handelman, he's right. Without the physical evidence, all the hell we've got are a bunch of confessions, and all of them 're conflicting. Give every one of those old folks a chance to testify, they'll admit everything from the Chicago fire to the Boston Strangler, and all stops in between. No way, Bro. I got to admit, though, it's a hell of an intriguing concept. Hey, you remember I told you about that thing I wrote in college, on laudable homicide? Well, here it is, bigger 'n shit. Only we can't do a thing about it. Hell of a choice, my man, we can either book 'em or hang a medal on 'em. Pity we can't do both somehow."

Lew unconsciously ran his fingertips up and down a crack in the steering wheel. "Hey, look," he said, "I don't want to go back to the station yet, without this thing resolved in my mind. It'd somehow be wrong to just break this thing, report what we've got and let somebody go down there with a paddy wagon and haul them all in, without knowing for sure what we're doing.

"For that matter, we know it couldn't have been all of them in there. How do we separate the sheep from the goats? Like old Handelman said, a week could be a life sentence for some of them, and that's just as bad as letting the guilty go. Hell, we try to separate the confessors from the shooters, we go round and round, maybe we get nowhere at all. We need time to think. Tell you what: they're not going anyplace, how about we radio in, go ten-seven for overnight, try to work out something between now and then. Maybe we buy us a little time, get us some answers. Right now, I just can't think of anything better to do. What do you think?"

"I think we don't call in at all. Turn the radio off, let 'em think it's broke again, and we just show up again tomorrow morning. Besides, this late, who'd care where we are?"

"God, I don't know," Lew said. "Yeah, let's do that." He reached for the radio knob and turned it to the "off" position. A droning voice that they had subconsciously monitored, listening for the key words that identified their unit, stopped in mid-call.

Dan picked up the thread of his thought: "Maybe we'll get half-smashed and some kind of inspiration'll come. I've got a mess of steaks over at my place." He looked around, focusing his eyes for the first time beyond the dash. "Look, we're only a couple of blocks from Smelzer's; let's drop over there, get us a case of beer, then head over to my place. You can call Mrs. Halloran from there, tell her to put dinner back into the fridge, then make excuses to your lady love. Turn left here."

* * * * * * * * * *

Epilogue

WHEN they had all gathered in the dayroom, Howard Kirk adjusted his glasses, cleared his throat, and began to read: "It says here on Page One, 'Two Policemen Slain in Shootout. Daniel Perkins, 37, and Lewis Perkins, 38, unrelated, died at Mercy Hospital this morning as a result of gunshot wounds suffered yesterday evening when they broke up an armed robbery in progress at Smelzer's Liquor Store, 4505 Barry. Two suspects were killed in the affray. However, Police Department sources indicated that yet another suspect may be at large, since one of the officers had been shot in the back from apparently close range. No witnesses to the incident were found ...' It goes on, but I don't think it's necessary for me to read it." Anger clouded his face. "You know, I liked those boys. I liked them." A general murmur of agreement ran through the room.

He reached down and took a domino from the stack on the table, and gently rapped it three times on the tabletop. "The meeting will now come to order ...."

AUTHOR'S NOTE

COPS, like firemen, are a very strange breed. They voluntarily do a job that others won't do, for less than others get, and know that while the job says they must go out there, it also says they do not necessarily have to come back. This is for every badge that ever fell L.O.D.

This is a work of fiction, and any similarities to persons living or dead or actual events is unintentional. However, a few of the idiosyncrasies of some badges I had the pleasure of working with have crept in to add a little flavor.

AUTHOR'S SECOND NOTE: This book was written and sent to the publisher before the events of September 11. When something of that magnitude happens, everyone who ever carried a badge of any organization feels the impact and has to do something about it. Accordingly, ten percent of the proceeds of this book will go toward the aid of the survivors of the police officers and firefighters who lost their lives LOD on that very dark day.